GETTING SOFT

Skye Fargo had told Charlie Sycamore what he'd do if the Indian scout came trailing him. He would kill him.

But maybe Fargo was getting soft. He had caught Charlie and hadn't pulled the trigger. He was letting Charlie walk away alive. But he warned the scout, "Don't think about taking your horse. I might change my mind."

Fargo was surprised when Charlie's hand darted toward his pistol. The scout was faster than he'd ever expected. But not fast enough.

Fargo's shot slammed into Charlie's chest, and the man flew backward as though he'd been kicked by a mule. The scout shuddered once and was still.

"Damn," Fargo said, "you should've quit while you were ahead."

And the Trailsman slowly holstered his gun, thinking that getting soft was an easy way to get dead. . . .

THE

TRAILSMAN

168

KIOWA
COMMAND

by

Jon Sharpe

A SIGNET BOOK

SIGNET
Published by the Penguin Group
Penguin Books USA Inc., 375 Hudson Street,
New York, New York 10014, U.S.A.
Penguin Books Ltd, 27 Wrights Lane,
London W8 5TZ, England
Penguin Books Australia Ltd, Ringwood,
Victoria, Australia
Penguin Books Canada Ltd, 10 Alcorn Avenue,
Toronto, Ontario, Canada M4V 3B2
Penguin Books (N.Z.) Ltd, 182–190 Wairau Road,
Auckland 10, New Zealand

Penguin Books Ltd, Registered Offices:
Harmondsworth, Middlesex, England

First published by Signet, an imprint of Dutton Signet,
a division of Penguin Books USA Inc.

First Printing, December, 1995
10 9 8 7 6 5 4 3 2 1

The Trailsman

Beginnings ... they bend the tree and they mark the man. Skye Fargo was born when he was eighteen. Terror was his midwife, vengeance his first cry. Killing spawned Skye Fargo, ruthless, cold-blooded murder. Out of the acrid smoke of gunpowder still hanging in the air, he rose, cried out a promise never forgotten.

The Trailsman they began to call him all across the West: searcher, scout, hunter, the man who could see where others only looked, his skills for hire but not his soul, the man who lived each day to the fullest, yet trailed each tomorrow. Skye Fargo, the Trailsman, and the seeker who could take the wildness of a land and the wanting of a woman and make them his own.

*1860, where the southwest territory,
a harsh, untamed, and vengeful land
is witness to a devil's bargain
of savagery and death . . .*

1

They were near. Not more than two ridges away, he estimated. The big man with the lake-blue eyes let a silent oath escape the tight line of his lips. He hadn't liked the job from its outset. Getting closer to the end of it didn't help any. He carried two reasons for disliking the assignment. He never enjoyed working for the army. They were always so damn heavy-handed. Instead of listening to those who knew better, they invariably bulled their way, too often losing their quarry and always unnecessarily losing lives. They probably couldn't help it, Skye Fargo told himself. The military mind was set in its ways, immovable and unimaginative, governed by rules and regulations, bogged down by outmoded tactical manuals designed for another time and another place.

Even a general as smart and flexible as Miles Stanford was not entirely able to free himself from indoctrinated rigidness, Fargo reflected unhappily. So much for the first reason for his general sourness. The second one was that he disliked trailing renegades, especially renegade Indians. They were as unpredictable as the army was predictable. In dealing with the Indian, it was vital to know the differences in tribal codes and tribal behavior. Those were things that could spell the difference between keeping your scalp and losing it. But renegades were outcasts. They had turned their back on their own people. They lived by their own formless rules, which were beyond knowing. Yet he was here, Fargo swore silently, thanks to General Miles Stanford. Damn the man, Fargo thought. He was an old friend who always found a way to prevail on him. Fargo pushed aside further complaining to scan the ground in front of him.

He had been trailing the band of renegades for more than three weeks, ever since he'd left General Stanford's headquarters on the border of the Colorado–New Mexico territory, and now he felt a grim satisfaction gather inside himself. They were indeed not far ahead, Fargo realized as he swung from the magnificent Ovaro to step carefully along the oblong stretch of ground beside a stand of blackjack oak. Skye Fargo studied the ground with the practiced and special eyes of a trailsman, seeing where others only looked, understanding what others failed to comprehend. The renegades had camped here, at least ten of them, he estimated. He first walked along the edge of the spot where they had tethered their horses.

He saw mostly unshod Indian pony prints, but spotted three sets of horseshoe hoofprints, horses taken from a settler or wagon train. He moved forward, scanning every mark, every indentation, every little depression of earth, grass, moss, and low brush. The earth, a combination of downy bromegrass, soft topsoil, and profuse weeds and moss, gave its secrets to those who knew how to unravel them. The renegades carried rifles, he noted as he took in the thin, long depressions in the grass where they'd laid the guns. Small holes in the ground showed him that half of them also carried lances that had been thrust into the soil to stand upright and ready for instant use. The men had slept apart from each other, a practice that carried its own message. They were wily, he thought, not without a grim appreciation. They practiced caution at all times. They'd not be targeted in a cluster.

Fargo knelt down and let his fingers sift through the grass still pressed down where the renegades had slept. As he moved from spot to spot, the little wisps of material came off on his fingers, linsey-woolsey caught on the edges of the grass, white man's wool. Blankets, he realized, taken from their victims. Letting his fingers continue to explore the soil where each of the Indians had slept, he found bits and pieces of berries, prairie turnips, and sunflower seeds, remains of their morning meal. But the meal leftovers were not at a camp meal spot. They were beside where each man had slept. Fargo nodded at the message that gave him.

The renegades were so cautiously crafty they took their meals separately, unwilling to risk being caught eating together in a group or sleeping together. Fargo rose, his jaw tight. But he had a better picture of his quarry now. They were clever, acting together as a band, dependent on each other yet fully prepared to act individually, each man complete in himself with weapons and food. It was no doubt the key to their raids and attacks. They struck together and fled singly, to regroup later at an agreed-upon spot. Fargo climbed onto the Ovaro and turned the horse southeast to find Lieutenant Elwood Siebert of Troop C, United States Cavalry, who had been following behind him for the past three weeks. Orders of General Miles Stanford, of course. Fargo let his thoughts go back to his last meeting with the general.

Miles Stanford had sent three corporals to find him, obviously aware he'd be at the Brady ranch as he brought Jack Brady's herd down from the Dakotas. The three soldiers escorted him to the general's headquarters at the bottom of Colorado territory, a small but sturdy stockade fort from which the army patrolled all the way into Utah territory. "You're looking fit as ever," Fargo had told Miles with admiration. He had indeed never seen General Miles Stanford when he didn't look fit. Stanford was a tall man with an imposing presence and prematurely silver hair in a young face. Miles was one of the better generals the army had sent into the untamed territories. "Of course, you didn't have your soldier boys bring me all the way down here because you miss me," Fargo slid at him as he took the glass of bourbon offered him.

Miles Stanford chuckled as he raised his glass. "No, but it's damn good seeing you," he said. "It's been a good spell since we worked together. You know I've always liked working with you, Fargo."

Fargo made a wry sound. "We've known each other too long for flattery. You've a problem or you wouldn't have dragged me down here."

"You're growing too cynical," the general returned. "But you're right, of course. I've a problem and it's called a rotten band of renegades. These are real bad actors, Fargo. They've been pulling off particularly brutal raids all over this territory. My patrols only find what they've left when they finish, which isn't much. I want to put a stop to them and I need you to find them."

Fargo finished the bourbon as he spoke. "How many?"

"Wouldn't know. No survivors around to tell. But the best guess is anywhere from eight to twelve," the general said.

Fargo screwed his face up. "Twelve's a lot for a band of renegades," he said.

"You're right, but I think they're maybe picking up more members each time. They've no pattern, no tribal roots, of course. But they keep crossing and crisscrossing the region. You could pick up a pattern and a trail.

You're the only one I know who could. Extra pay for this one, old friend," Miles Stanford said, and let himself look hopeful.

"What am I supposed to do if I find them? Take them on all by myself, or come back here to report to you? They'll be on their way by the time I do that," Fargo said.

"I'm sending a patrol to follow along behind you," the general said.

"Far behind me," Fargo grunted.

"Far as you want," Miles said. "You find them, you go and get them, and they'll do the rest. I'm going to send Lieutenant Elwood Siebert to take the patrol. He's young but he's got good training. He's out of the academy."

"Which means he's standard-issue army shavetail," Fargo grunted. "Long on manuals, short on experience."

The general's lips tightened for a moment but he made no protest, and Fargo allowed a grim snort to escape him. "I've told him about you. He's properly impressed," Miles said.

"Thanks, but what's that mean?" Fargo queried.

"He won't interfere with you. He'll take it slow as you want, stay back as far as you want, stop if you want him to stop. But he'll be there and ready when you need him. Of course, it'd be nice if you checked back with him once in a while."

"I haven't even agreed to do this, and you've got me checking back with him," Fargo protested.

"I expect you'll agree, old friend. I know you don't like renegades. Besides, I've something to sweeten the pot for you."

"Such as?" Fargo inquired.

"A real easy job at top dollar. By the time you get back, I expect a man named Burroughs to be here with two wagons of oriental silks he wants to get to the Missouri at St.

Louis. He wrote ahead for an army scout. I can't give him one, of course, but I can give him you. It's a nice, clean job, and as I said, he's offering top dollar. It's all yours. That sweet enough?" the general said, plainly pleased with his bargain.

"I guess so," Fargo conceded, and the general rose at once.

"Be right back. I want you to meet Lieutenant Siebert," he said, hurrying from the office to return moments later with a very young, tall, and ramrod-stiff junior officer in a sharply creased uniform. Fargo took in clear blue eyes, blondish hair cropped short, and an unlined face that tried to let serious earnestness take the place of maturity.

"Glad to meet you, Sir," the lieutenant said with a crisp salute. "I look forward to riding with you."

Fargo groaned inwardly. "We won't be doing much riding together, Lieutenant," he said. Then, softening his answer, he added, "But I'll be depending on you when I'm ready." Elwood Siebert continued to look seriously earnest.

"You can count on me," he said, and left the room with a snappy salute to the general.

"He'll do fine. He's a good young officer," the general said to Fargo when they were alone.

"Make sure he knows I'm calling the shots," Fargo grunted.

"Be ready to leave within the hour," Miles had said with a nod.

That had been the start of it, Fargo thought to himself as he clicked the pictures from his mind. He returned his eyes to the two ridges as he moved through a line of box elder, away from the ridges and down into a tree-covered gully. He continued to ride southeast and climbed out of the gully as his gaze moved along the horizon line. He had told the lieutenant to ride slowly. No dust plumes, he'd said, and now he had to live with that instruction. Slowly, he scanned each stretch of box elder, hawthorn, and blackjack oak and silently swore as the sun moved higher into the sky. He found a high promontory that afforded a falcon's view of the countryside and surveyed every direction. Then he caught the movement he searched for—branches being swayed in a straight line.

Putting the pinto into a gallop, he sent the horse downward, raced through trees and open spaces, and slowed only when he came in sight of the column of blue-clad riders. The lieutenant rode at the head of the eighteen troopers and brought the column to a halt as Fargo rode up. "Found them," Fargo said, and Lieutenant Siebert's face filled with eager anticipation. "Couple of hours north," Fargo said as he swung the Ovaro around and began to lead the way. He slowed to a halt when they reached the second rise, and the lieutenant drew alongside him. "They're an hour or so past the next rise," Fargo said.

"That's all we need," Elwood Siebert said confidently.

"For what?" Fargo queried.

"To catch them on the run," the lieutenant said.

"You can't do that," Fargo said.

"Why not?" Siebert frowned.

"They'll hear you and see you. They'll take off," Fargo said.

"We'll be on them before they can get away. Our horses can outrun their short-legged ponies," Siebert said.

Fargo shook his head. "It won't work. You'll lose them all. These bastards won't act the way ordinary Indians would. An ordinary Indian band might decide to fight or run or both. But whatever they decided they'd do as a unit. Not these. These aren't ordinary Indians. These are renegades, mister. They won't be fighting like ordinary Indians."

"You've a plan in mind, I take it," Siebert said with undisguised deprecation in his tone.

"Go a little further, get a little closer on horseback, then dismount and close in on them on foot after they've settled down. Sneak up on them on foot and split your men into two groups," Fargo said.

He saw the lieutenant's frown turn into chiding tolerance. "Mister Fargo, this is the United States Cavalry. The cavalry doesn't attack on foot."

"It better this time," Fargo said grimly.

"Nonsense," Siebert said, and Fargo silently swore at the youthful arrogance in the officer's face. "Our horses can outrun those short-legged Indian ponies. We'll get them before they can scatter very far."

"Hell you will," Fargo snapped.

Siebert's face stayed infuriatingly smug. "I've made a specialty of pursuit-and-destroy operations. I know exactly how we'll get them. You are an outstanding trailsman, my dear man, but I'm afraid you're not a very good judge of military tactics."

"I'm a damn good judge of renegade tactics. You chase them your way and you'll get nothing except casualties," Fargo insisted.

The lieutenant's smile remained chiding. "You found them for us. We'll do the rest. You watch. I promise you results," he said.

"I'll make you a promise. I promise not to laugh," Fargo said and saw Siebert's lips tighten as he wheeled his horse to his troopers.

"Troop forward at the gallop," the lieutenant shouted and raced away.

"Shit," Fargo muttered, swerving the Ovaro as the troopers thundered past him. He rode the pinto at an angle, entered a stand of blackjack oak, and stayed in it as the lieutenant led his men up a passageway. Staying inside the trees, he stayed to the right of the passage and let the Ovaro go full out, finally passing the troopers, as they had to slow when the passage narrowed and grew thick with foliage. He crested the rise, still going full out, confident of the Ovaro's powerful hindquarters, which gave him an agility the lieutenant's horses didn't possess. He drew away from the line of troopers and was a good hundred yards ahead of them when they crested the rise and found another open pathway. Riding hard, he stayed in the wooded terrain and glimpsed enough open land for the troopers to take. The renegades had taken the open passages, too, he was certain, and he estimated that almost an hour had passed when he glimpsed the small band of near-naked riders moving through a break of five-foot-tall goosefoot.

Staying in the tree cover, he passed the Indians, slowing to a trot as he peered through the leaves. They were riding casually. He glimpsed an Osage armband, a rawhide vest on another with what was very definitely Cheyenne bead-work, and a pouch carried by still another with a Kansa scroll design painted onto the leather. A tall renegade with long black hair rode slightly ahead of the others, his face long and lean with the heavy features of the Pawnee. Fargo edged still further ahead. His eyes were on the renegades when he saw them suddenly stiffen and turn around on their ponies.

They had picked up the sound of the troopers. Fargo reined the pinto to a halt and leaped from the saddle, taking the big Henry from its saddle case. He held the rifle in one hand as he watched the Indians drop from their mounts and instantly separate, each man going into the tree cover beyond the goosefoot passage. His eyes were on the tall, lean one with the long black hair and the Pawnee face. He saw the renegade lead his pony into the trees and then drop onto one knee, a rifle in his hands. He glimpsed another of the renegades some ten yards away, also melting into the trees. Glancing across the passage, he was able to catch a glimpse of two more of the renegades, apart from each other, as they sank down into the tree cover. Fargo cursed silently. They were going to do exactly what he'd expected, exactly what they had practiced doing. They'd fire one volley, maybe two, cut down at least six or so troopers, and then race away through the trees on both sides, each man moving separately, entirely apart from the others.

They'd let the troopers catch a glimpse of them, lure them into giving chase before they scattered like milkweed seeds. They'd disappear in all directions, each man a self-sufficient entity, needing neither to hunt for food nor depend on someone else. Someplace, they had a prearranged place to meet. Fargo lifted the rifle to his shoulder. He couldn't let them all vanish untouched. He'd take down at least one, perhaps the leader. That could be more than enough to destroy the band. His finger rested on the rifle trigger as the lieutenant charged into view with his troops. One of the renegades rose into sight on the other side of the passage.

The lieutenant reined his mount in at once, started to turn with his troops, when the volley of shots exploded from both sides of the passage. Six of the troopers went down, and Fargo saw two others clutch at their sides as they managed to stay on their horses. The renegade across the way dropped out of view as the rest of the troop milled in confusion and tried to take cover. Fargo's eyes moved to the lean-faced Indian as the red man leaped onto his pony and started to race away. He lay flat against his mount's back, but Fargo's sights were already following him. The big

Henry erupted, a single shot, and the renegade fell sideways from his pony, one side of his head disappearing in a shower of red.

Fargo had already swung the rifle before the man hit the ground, catching sight of another of the renegades racing away. Once again, the rifle barked and the renegade toppled from his mount. Fargo whirled at the sound to his rear and was in time to see another of the Indians racing through the trees. He swung the Henry in a half-circle, fired again, two shots this time, and saw the figure fall backward from the horse's back. Fargo returned his eyes to the passage, where the troopers were trying to chase down the other renegades, riding wildly from side to side in the trees, some firing meaningless shots. The Indians had already disappeared, charging away through the trees, each figure alone, a will-o'-the-wisp flash glimpsed for but a brief moment. The troopers were still charging through the trees in aimless pursuit as Fargo rose to his feet and walked to the Ovaro.

He led the Ovaro out of the trees by the reins and stopped where the lieutenant sat his horse, his eyes filled with shock, his young face suddenly older. "It was all so fast," Elwood Siebert murmured, his voice hollow.

"You never got a chance to use those military tactics the manuals taught you," Fargo said. He peered at the lieutenant's haggard face. "It happens that way out here, son," he said, and Siebert's eyes stared back. "You grow up all of a sudden." The lieutenant swallowed hard as the other troopers began straggling back.

"They got away, every damn one of them," one of the soldiers said with bitterness coating his words.

"Three of them didn't," Fargo said. "You'll find them in the trees back there. One of them might have been their leader. If so, that could be the end of them."

"How'll we know?" Siebert asked.

"We won't," Fargo said. "Not for a while."

"How long would it take you to track down the rest of them?" the lieutenant asked.

"A month, maybe two. Too long. This mission's over. Go back and report," Fargo said.

"You're not coming?" Siebert asked.

"In a few days. I want a little time," Fargo said.

"To get over my not listening to you," Siebert said.

"That's part of it. To get over losing. I don't like losing," Fargo said.

"I'll tell General Stanford it was my fault," the lieutenant said, a little stiffly.

"Never expected you wouldn't," Fargo said honestly. The younger man's nod said that he understood and was grateful for the trust. One of the troopers told the lieutenant they'd suffered four killed. Fargo swung onto the Ovaro and rode away and felt the bitterness claw at him. It hadn't been his fault, but that didn't help any. That just let him avoid feeling guilty. Bitterness came with the knowing that things could turn wrong so quickly in this land. It was a feeling he knew only one way to drown, and he turned the horse north. A tiny cluster of buildings that had the effrontery to call itself a town lay but a day's ride into Colorado territory. Ellie Smith lived there. Leastways she had two years ago. He expected she still did. Ellie had never been the roving kind. He let memories quicken the pace as he rode.

It was afternoon the next day when he reached Ellie Smith's place, a little house and a small patch of land where she grew vegetables and baked biscuits and pies for the equally small travelers' inn nearby. She exploded with delight when she saw him ride to a halt and was hanging onto him in seconds. They talked of old times and old moments into the night, and when they lay naked together it was as if there had been no years in between. Ellie Smith had always been one of those women who carried ten to fifteen pounds extra and looked the better for it. Ellie was a creature of roundness, round face more pleasant than pretty, round shoulders, round breasts made for caressing, soft round ass made for enjoying, not a single angular, sharp line to her. Ellie's personality matched her physical self, a clear case of the flesh and the spirit borrowing from each other.

Ellie was exactly what he needed, no pretense to her, no false coyness, not ever, just wonderful, enveloping warmth. The round breasts were magnificent pillows against his face and he reveled in their cushioned warmth, in tasting of the full red-brown nipples that seemed to epitomize Ellie's frank womanliness. "Yes, yes, oh, God, so long . . . so damn long," Ellie gasped out as his hard-muscled body came against the round little belly. She thrust herself upward, moving the dark, wiry triangle against his crotch, pressing, seeking, and then screaming as his own firm warmth slid into her. Memories flowed over Fargo, the past mingling with the present, all the enveloping passions echoing again, today made sweeter by yesterday.

He enjoyed Ellie through the night, as she enjoyed him, until they finally slept through the beginning of the new day. When she woke, he enjoyed watching her unselfconscious radiance as she stayed naked as she prepared breakfast. He stayed two more days and nights with Ellie, time in which it seemed they both tried to encompass all of today and tomorrow. Finally he lay with her, exhausted but in that special way of pure sensual communication cleansed, the bitterness gone from him. "Don't wait another two years," Ellie said to him as he prepared to leave.

"I'll try not to," he told her. Ellie would hold him to that, he knew, even as she realized it was no promise. He left then, having thanked Ellie more than he had words to say. He turned the Ovaro southeast and headed for Miles Stanford's stockade.

2

He expected Miles Stanford to be waiting with both impatience and irritation when he returned to the compound. The slender figure in the office was indeed impatient and irritated, but that's where the similarity ended. Fargo found himself staring at hair the color of newly shucked corn, worn full and loose around a face of handsome but angular beauty. He took in dark blue eyes with very clear whites, arching eyebrows, a straight, thin nose, and lips a little narrow yet finely etched. The irritation was undisguised in the young woman's face, the arching eyebrows adding a note of arrogant annoyance.

He took in a long, graceful neck that led down to a white shirt covering longish breasts that were nonetheless nicely filled at the bottoms. Narrow-hipped, with long legs encased in a black skirt that showed nicely turned calves, she exuded an air of command as well as irritation. Her eyes scanned him with a frown of dark blue intensity. "You're Fargo," she said, crisply.

"Bull's-eye. How'd you know?" he said quietly.

Her eyes swept across his strong, chiseled features and the big, taut frame. "You fit the general's description," she said.

Fargo nodded back. "Whose description do you fit, honey?" he asked.

"Jessica Winter. I've been waiting five damn weeks for you. You were supposed to return with Lieutenant Siebert. Why didn't you?" she thrust angrily at him.

"That's none of your damn business," Fargo said.

"I'm afraid it is. You stayed away almost another entire week. Visiting some woman, I'll wager," Jessica Winter said, disapproval in her tone.

"That'd be a good wager," Fargo said affably.

Jessica Winter let a half-snort pass her lips, and the disapproval held in her handsome face. "I suppose I should be grateful. You've gotten it out of your system," she said.

"Jessica, honey, getting laid is like breathing. You never get it out of your system, not till you die, and that's the way it was planned out to be," Fargo said.

"Some men can discipline their urges," she sniffed.

"Some men can pass a trumpet honeysuckle and not stop to look," Fargo said. "Now, where in hell is the general?"

"He's in the field. He'll be back tonight," she said.

"Good," Fargo nodded, turned on his heel, and started for the door.

"Just a second, Fargo," Jessica Winter said, her tone commanding. "You're not just walking away after I've been waiting all this time."

He halted, turned to fasten his lake-blue eyes on her, again took in the narrow-hipped, long slenderness of her loveliness. "You want to tell me why not?" he slid at her.

"Because you'll be working for me. I'm hiring you," she said with cool imperiousness.

Fargo paused and allowed a calm smile to touch his lips. "I think you'd best lay off the peyote, Jessica," he said calmly.

"I haven't had any peyote," she snapped. "But I have been talking to General Stanford. He'll verify what I've said."

"The hell he will," Fargo threw back.

"He said you might be uncooperative," Jessica remarked somewhat indulgently.

"That's only a sample, doll," Fargo said as he strode from the office. She followed him outside as he took the Ovaro and started to lead the horse away.

"You'll change your attitude. Money has a way of convincing people to change their attitudes," Jessica Winter said.

Fargo paused and fastened her with a narrowed glance. "You've a lot of nerve to go with your attitude, I'll give you that," he said and strode away. He felt her watching him as he led the Ovaro to a halt outside one of the small shacks that served the compound as guest quarters. He tethered the horse and went into the shack, shed his jacket, and stretched out on the lone cot, his long frame hanging over the edge of one end. He closed his eyes, half dozed, and was sorry he hadn't stayed longer with Ellie. When the day drifted into dusk, he came awake at the sound of hoofbeats and then voices and the rattle of rein chains. Rising, he glanced out the doorway to see the troop leading their horses into the stables. He saw Siebert already on his way to the officers' quarters as a trooper led his horse away.

Fargo glanced away just in time to see Miles Stanford disappear into his office. Pulling his jacket on, Fargo headed for the general's office and saw Jessica Winter start from the door of one of the guest shacks, halt, and wait. He strode into Miles Stanford's quarters and saw the general's eyes lift as he stormed in. "I see you met Jessica Winter," the general said. Fargo halted in surprise.

"You assuming?" Fargo asked.

"No. I'm looking. I see you're all steamed. She has a way of doing that," the general said.

"You can say that again. Who the hell is she?" Fargo questioned.

"The favorite niece of Senator Ted Winter, United States Congress," Miles said. "It seems the senator came out to Colorado territory on some kind of mission and disappeared. She came to find him."

"How'd I get into it?" Fargo frowned.

General Stanford screwed up his face and looked uncomfortable. "Well, that sort of came about," he said.

"Just how?" Fargo frowned.

"She came with a letter from Washington ordering me to help her. I told her if there was anyone who could find her uncle it was you. She's been waiting for you to get back here."

"Then what's all this shit about my working for her?"

The general looked more uncomfortable. "She came here well briefed. She knows I have the authority to direct any civilian in the territory to follow my orders. She flat out told me she expected me to do just that."

"Jesus, Miles, you intend to do that?" Fargo asked in disbelief.

"You know I wouldn't do that unless I was desperate, not after all the times we've worked together," the general said. "But she does have me over a barrel on this, and she's a very determined young woman."

"You telling me to go work for her? No way, Miles. I've a nice long haul for Tom Schramm waiting for me. Besides, when did you start worrying about what Washington thinks?"

"I'm not. I just want you to hear her out. That way she can't say I didn't try," Miles Stanford grumbled.

"What happened to the feller with the oriental silks?" Fargo asked.

"I'm afraid that job came to a sudden end. Got a message

that his wagons broke down and fell into the South Platte, ruined all his silks," the general said.

"No matter to me. It would've been on my way to Tom Schramm in Jefferson City. Now I'll go straight down to Tom. He wants me to break trail for him all the way down into the Pecos," Fargo said.

"You see the lieutenant when he came back?" the general queried, and Fargo shook his head no. "He told me what happened. He's still shaken by it. He should've listened to you and he's learned. He'll be a good officer someday."

"I'm glad, for him and for you," Fargo said.

"Now, go talk to Jessica Winter. Give her your answer and I'll wrestle with the rest. She'll be real mad, you can count on that," the general said. "She really wants to find her uncle and she's not the kind to take kindly to being turned down."

"Then it's time she learned that," Fargo said as he walked from the office with a nod. He saw the tall, slender figure waiting outside in the remaining dusk, the corn-yellow hair still bright even in the fading light. The arched eyebrows completed the smug arrogance in her face.

"Ready to go to work for me now, Fargo?" Jessica Winter said.

"How long has the senator been missing?" Fargo asked, ducking the question.

"Four months since he was last heard from," Jessica said. "We received a note in Washington."

"He say where he was?" Fargo inquired.

"Near a place called Alamosa," she said.

Fargo let a snort escape his lips. "It'd be a wild-goose chase and I don't like wild-goose chases. It's ninety-nine percent sure your uncle's no longer alive. I'm sorry, but that's the hard truth of it."

He saw the flash of pain touch her dark blue eyes, but her chin lifted at once and her lips tightened. "That leaves one percent. That's enough for me," she said. "I'm sure the general told you I'll pay triple the usual rate for your services."

"He didn't tell me and it doesn't make any difference. I've another job waiting. Do yourself a favor and go home, Jessica."

"That's out of the question. You have your orders. You're going to help me. The subject's not open for debate," she said haughtily, thin eyebrows arching again.

"I don't have any orders and I'm cutting out of here come morning. That's not open for debate, either," Fargo said and saw Jessica Winter's brows lower into a frown.

"Are you telling me the general didn't requisition you?" she tossed at him.

"I'm telling you the general knows a requisition isn't worth steer shit," Fargo said.

"We'll see about that," she hissed, spun on her heel, and strode toward the general's quarters.

Fargo went on his way to where the Ovaro waited outside the guest shack. He unsaddled the horse, took his gear into the shack with him, shed his jacket and shirt, and stretched out on the cot. He would have felt concern for some junior officer facing Jessica Winter, but Miles Stanford was made of steel and experience under his proper facade. He might even have felt some sympathy for Jessica, but he always found it hard being sympathetic to arrogance and imperiousness. He was wondering if he'd get another visit from her when the door flew open and the slender figure strode into the shack.

He saw Jessica pause for a moment as her eyes fastened on his smoothly muscled torso, and then the blazing fury returned to the dark blue orbs. "I've never been so disappointed in anyone," she flung at him.

"Sorry about that," Fargo said calmly.

"Not you," she snapped. "You're simply selfish and insensitive. I'm talking about General Stanford. He's an officer and a gentleman. I expected more from him. He's obviously allowing you to go your way and that's disgraceful. I'm going to report his actions to Washington."

"Good luck," Fargo said, and she glared at him. "That all you stopped back here to tell me?"

"No. It's apparent I can't appeal to your sensitivity or decency. I'll try appealing to your loyalty."

"Loyalty?" he questioned.

"To General Stanford. It's plain you're very good friends. You can save him from getting a severe reprimand in Washington if I report his lack of cooperation. You can prevent that."

Fargo gave her a wide smile. "Nice try, Jessica," he said. "But Miles can fight his own battles." He watched tight-lipped anger shape her face as he turned at the sound just outside the door and saw the general there.

"Sorry to interrupt, but there's somebody else to see you, Fargo," Miles Stanford said.

"Who?" Fargo frowned.

"Charlie Sycamore," the general said.

Fargo's frown dug deeper into his brow. "What the hell does Charlie Sycamore want with me?"

"He wouldn't say, but he's been hanging around waiting for weeks. What with talking about Miss Winter's problems, I forgot to tell you. He's waiting just inside the stockade gate," the general said.

"I'll go see what he wants," Fargo nodded.

"Fill me in later," the general said as he hurried away.

"Someone else for you to turn down?" Fargo heard Jessica ask, ice in her voice.

"You can pretty damn well count on it," Fargo said as she followed him from the shack.

"Charlie Sycamore. What an unusual name," she commented.

"He's what they call a breed out here."

"What's that?" she questioned.

"An Indian with mixed blood, usually white, but sometimes Mexican or Negro," Fargo told her. "Charlie Sycamore's Kiowa with some Kansa and Mexican blood. You can't trust him much, but he's a smart scout. He keeps his ear out and he'll sell valuable information for the right price. General Stanford has used him, along with a lot of other commanders."

"Even though he's untrustworthy?"

"Sometimes he has the skill and the information needed."

"My God, doesn't anyone take a moral stand out here?" she asked with indignant righteousness.

"Sure, all the time," Fargo said, "after you get through doing your job and staying alive."

He turned and walked on to halt where the figure waited near the stockade gate. Charlie Sycamore was clothed in black as always, Fargo noted—black Levi's, short black jacket, shapeless black hat, and black kerchief around his long, thin neck. An angular figure, he wore long, thick strands of greased black hair that fell around his dark-complexioned face. His almost opaque blue eyes always seemed out of place in his thin face. Standing very still, Charlie Sycamore was a figure that somehow managed to radiate the contradictory qualities of cunning and ingenuousness.

"Hello, Charlie," Fargo said, and the scout nodded back. "Talk," Fargo said.

"I bring message. Great Chief wants you to come," Charlie Sycamore said.

"What great chief?"

"Great Kiowa Chief Red Hawk," the scout said.

Fargo's eyes narrowed at once. "Red Hawk is not a great chief. He's a snake-tongued, murdering, massacring butcher."

"Red Hawk says I bring you to him," the scout said.

"Why?" Fargo frowned.

"He will tell you. You will be safe. He gives his word," Charlie Sycamore said.

"His word is shit," Fargo snapped.

"He gave word on sign of his fathers. I see him," the scout said.

"I've nothing to say to him," Fargo returned.

"He says you come."

"Is Red Hawk ready to stop burning down cabins, torturing, raping, and murdering helpless men, women, and children? Is he ready to stop slaughtering wagon trains? Did he tell his warriors to put down their weapons?" Fargo asked and received only a stony silence. He uttered a grim snort. "Didn't think so. Tell him when he's ready to do that I'll come see him," Fargo finished.

"Red Hawk says you come with me now," the scout said.

"Fargo says you and the chief can go to hell, Charlie," Fargo answered blandly.

"You make mistake, Fargo," Charlie Sycamore said, his face stiffening.

"I've made plenty. One more won't matter," Fargo said and watched the thin figure turn and walk from the stockade gate to where a light tan quarter horse waited. Not glancing back, the Indian swung onto the horse and rode into the night. When he was gone from sight, Fargo turned and saw Jessica there, the light from the torch on the stockade wall bathing her in a flickering glow.

"You're being consistent, at least," she said.

"Pardon me if I don't say thanks," Fargo answered.

"That was a strange request. Aren't you at all curious about why the chief wanted to see you?" Jessica asked.

"Sure I am, but I'm not about to risk my scalp to find out. Red Hawk is one of the most vicious, bloodthirsty chiefs in the territory, even for a Kiowa. I can't figure any reason he'd want to see me that'd do me any good," Fargo said.

Jessica Winter fell into step beside him, and suddenly in the flickering torchlight, the icy arrogance was gone from her. The sudden softness gave her a new beauty, an added weapon, perhaps, he reflected. "Perhaps I've come on a little strong," she said.

"Perhaps?" he cut in.

She shot him a quick glance that flared for an instant with the old arrogant fury and then softened. "All right, no perhaps. But I'd like to start over. I want to appeal to your conscience. It's the only thing I've left. Please listen."

"You've got till we get to my shack," Fargo said.

"A fine, decent, God-fearing man is missing, perhaps being tortured every day, or perhaps already dead. Doesn't that mean anything to you? It seems you're the only one with a chance of finding out what's happened to him. Can you just walk away from that? Maybe the money isn't that important to you, but what about your obligation as a human being?"

Her eyes pleaded more than pierced this time, and he stopped, faced her, and put his hands on her shoulders. There was no way to avoid the harshness of reality, but he kept the harshness out of his voice. "The obligations of a human being are a little different out here, Jessica. You want me to go on a wild-goose chase because he's your uncle, someone you care deeply about, and a fine person. Well, you can't chase down every well-meaning damn fool. You see, this land is full of good, decent, God-fearing people who've been massacred. This ground is stained forever with the blood of good families whose only crime was to want a place to settle. This is a cruel, hard land. Your uncle is just one more on a long list. You help those you've a chance of helping. The others are past helping. You don't have the strength to do more and there's not enough time in the world to help all those who needed help."

"You want me to go back and forget about it," she accused.

"I didn't say anything about forgetting. I'm saying go home and wait. At least you'll have memories if you're alive," he told her. The dark blue eyes bored into him for a long moment and gave no sign he had reached her. Finally, she pressed her lips tight, turned on her heel, and walked away. She held her back very straight, firm, tight rear hardly moving yet somehow strangely sensuous, as when the veiled is more powerful than the unveiled.

He watched her disappear into one of the shacks and then took the few dozen long strides to the general's office. "I'll be damned," Miles Stanford said when Fargo finished recounting the meeting with Charlie Sycamore. "What'd it mean?"

"Damned if I know," Fargo said.

"He's heard of you, but that's no surprise in this country. You've a reputation," the general said.

"And I sure know about him. I've seen enough of his victims," Fargo said, his voice angering at once.

"You think it was a trick to get hold of you? He have a special hate for you?" Miles asked.

"I don't know, but it's sure possible," Fargo said, rising to his feet. "I'll be leaving first thing come morning," he said. "It's a good ride down to Tom Schramm."

"Take care, old friend. I'll be calling on you again, I'm sure," the general said.

"I'd bet on it," Fargo laughed and left after a warm handshake. Stretched out on the cot in the shack, he wondered again about the strange visit from Charlie Sycamore and came up with no reasons for it so finally pushed the riddle aside. Jessica Winter swam into his thoughts and he found himself hoping he had managed to reach her. She was in a land she didn't understand, driven by care for her uncle and her own inner imperiousness. That was a deadly combination. It made for mistakes, replacing reason with wishful thinking and arrogance for judgment. Perhaps the general would be able to talk sense to her before she left, Fargo mused as he closed his eyes and drew sleep around himself.

He let himself take an extra hour when morning dawned. Then he rose, washed and dressed, and took the time to give the Ovaro a quick grooming with a body brush and hoof pick. He saddled up when he finished and walked the horse to the gate. His eyes swept the compound, aware that he was looking for a glimpse of the corn-silk hair, but he saw only Miles Stanford step from his quarters. "You see her this morning?" Fargo asked.

"She rode out at dawn. The watch sergeant told me. She had a horse, a tan gelding she bought in Trinity when she got off the stage. I guess she decided to head back," the general said.

"Good. Guess some of what I said stuck to her." Fargo nodded and waved as he rode from the compound. He headed east outside the gate, but stayed in the good, rich country of the Colorado territory, heavy with thick clusters of black walnut and box elder. He found a stand of pecans and stopped to enjoy the long, pointed nuts before going on. There was no need to hurry and he rode leisurely through the lush, throbbing foliage, letting himself pause often to enjoy the fields of brilliant cardinal flowers with their loose spires of brilliant red and the long stretches of pure white Indian pipes with their translucent white stems.

He was enjoying the slow leisure of the ride when suddenly he felt the hairs on the back of his neck grow stiff. He was not alone, said the warning transmitted to him by the Ovaro. He thought at once of what an old friend, Jake Smalley, used to say with the true wisdom of the stockman. Horses and women are the only critters that'll tell you all sorts of things without saying a word, Jake always said, and Fargo had come to learn the truth of that. A woman could do it with a flick of her eyes, by the way she set her lips or held her shoulders, sometimes by silence, sometimes by the swing of her hips. A horse told you things by the way it shook its head, by the movement of its ears, by the tightening of its neck or a sudden quick tattoo of its hooves.

Fargo saw the horse's ears were flicking forward, sideways, then forward again, and he rested a hand against one side of the powerful jet-black neck. "Easy, now," he barely whispered while his eyes scanned the thick foliage on both sides of where he rode. He spied the motion of the tree branches at his right, a line of movement. With a quick glance he saw the branches move at his left. Moments later, the two riders came into sight, both half-naked, one wearing an armband with Kiowa beadwork. He glanced to his right and saw two more Indians appear. Both pairs of riders were on ground slightly higher than where he rode, but he had open patches of terrain while they were in heavy foliage.

Drawing the Colt from its holster, Fargo dug heels into the pinto and the horse shot forward. Flattening himself forward on the horse's neck, Fargo raced around a cluster of red cedar and tossed a glance at the two Kiowa to his right. The Indians were charging down the small hill. Another glance showed the two riders on his left also streaking down to give chase. But Fargo had a half-dozen yards on both sets of attackers and he increased the distance as the Ovaro shot through a straight path between the trees. He stayed low on the horse, let the Ovaro gather its long stride, and raced forward. A line of near-naked horsemen suddenly stretched out in front of him.

"Shit," Fargo swore as he reined the Ovaro in, turned the horse to the left, and started to streak to the side. The two Kiowa came in from his left, angling to cut him off, and Fargo raised the Colt, fired off two shots, and one of the Kiowa flew from his saddleless pony. The other Indian swerved his mount, and Fargo raced the Ovaro in a straight line up the slope, aware the others were swinging in behind him. But the Ovaro's powerful hindquarters drove him forward, again lengthening the distance between himself and his pursuers. Fargo kept the horse racing in a straight line, dodging trees, and he had just crossed over the top of the slope when four more Kiowa emerged from the trees directly in front of him.

Again Fargo reined up, whirled the horse in a tight circle, and with a curse saw the line of pursuers was too close. Another pair of Kiowa came into sight in front of him. He kept the Colt in his hand as he pulled the Ovaro to a halt and watched the Indians form a circle around him. They had been positioned, waiting and watching from inside the woods. Fargo held the Ovaro still as the Kiowa kept him surrounded. He was scanning the near-naked figures when he saw the movement beyond the circle and another rider emerged from the trees, this one clad entirely in black, his eyes an opaque blue mask.

"Put away your gun, Fargo," Charlie Sycamore said. "You have already killed one of Red Hawk's braves."

"It happens when I'm being run down," Fargo said.

"We have not come for killing," Charlie Sycamore said. "We come to take you to Red Hawk."

Fargo swore inwardly. He was encircled and outnumbered, odds beyond fighting his way out. He'd buy time, he thought to himself, and dropped the Colt into its holster. Charlie Sycamore beckoned to him and led the way through the others, who fell in beside and behind him. Fargo rode in silence and smiled inwardly as he was led up slopes and down inclines, taken in long circles and criss-cross patterns in an obvious effort to confuse him. But Fargo kept mental notes as they rode, imprinting each important mark in his mind. The day had slid into late afternoon and a long stand of box elder stretched westward as Charlie Sycamore led the way through the timber.

Fargo heard the sound of running water before he caught sight of the Kiowa camp and a wide, fast-moving stream. He rode into the camp with Charlie Sycamore, saw a half-dozen tipis, a dozen bare-breasted squaws, and naked children, along with another handful of braves. The camp ended abruptly against a panel of trees, the stream running alongside it, the foliage a high green wall. Charlie Sycamore halted, motioned to Fargo, and the trailsman dismounted. He stood beside the Ovaro as the flap of the tallest tipi opened and the figure strode out.

Bare-chested, powerfully built, with long-muscled thighs below a dark blue breechclout, the chief halted before him. Fargo took in a stern, commanding face with heavy cheekbones and protruding brows that gave him a perpetual frown. Thick black hair, heavily coated with bear grease, was pulled back from his face, and a long necklace of hawk's claws hung around his neck, each curved talon strung together with thin rawhide. The chief's eyes, so dark they seemed black, pierced into him with a gaze that held burning appraisal, curiosity, and hate. Fargo returned the Indian's gaze with calm defiance that took more courage than sincerity, saying absolutely nothing. Charlie Sycamore's voice finally broke the silence.

"Red Hawk, Great Chief of the Kiowa," the scout said.

Fargo continued to remain silent, aware that the chief would understand the contempt in the silence. The scout spoke again and Fargo heard the uneasiness in his voice. "You speak Kiowa, Fargo?" he asked.

Fargo knew Siouan fairly well, some Shoshonean, and some Algonquian. He had a rudimentary acquaintance with the Caddoan and the Athabascan. Most all the tribes spoke one or the other of those major languages, but not the Kiowa. They had their own distinct language. "No," he answered, though he did understand a smattering.

"I will talk for Red Hawk and for you," Charlie Sycamore said, then spoke quickly to the chief, who nodded and fastened his eyes on Fargo again. As he spoke, Charlie Sycamore translated and Fargo listened without changing his expression.

"Red Hawk knows about the Trailsman," the chief said. "It is told you can fight like a wolf, ride like the wind, and track like an Apache."

"Better than an Apache," Fargo said as the scout instantly translated.

"The Trailsman has killed many Indian," Red Hawk said.

"Red Hawk has killed many white men, women, and children," Fargo answered, his tone hard.

The chief's eyes narrowed for a moment. "So it has been. So it will be," he said. "But for now, it will be different."

"How?" Fargo questioned.

"Now you will trail for Red Hawk," the chief said, and

Fargo felt the astonishment course through him. He looked incredulously at Charlie Sycamore.

"He's got to be kidding," Fargo said.

"Red Hawk does not make jokes," the scout said.

"Tell him I just turned down somebody a helluva lot better looking than him," Fargo said to Charlie Sycamore.

"You don't make jokes, either," the scout said in English, aimed only at his ears.

"Then tell him I don't work for murderers," Fargo said, and the scout translated, then quickly relayed the Kiowa chief's answer.

"Red Hawk says you will trail for him," Charlie Sycamore said, paused, and then spoke to him again. "I hear yellow-hair woman talk to the general. You turn her down. You do not turn down Red Hawk."

"If I want to stay alive," Fargo bit out.

"Not you alone," the scout said.

"What the hell does that mean?" Fargo demanded.

"Listen to Red Hawk," Charlie Sycamore said, spoke to the Kiowa chief, and then translated the Indian's answer.

"You, Trailsman, you will trail for me, Chief of the Kiowa," Red Hawk said imperiously. "You will find my daughter and bring her back to me."

Fargo felt the astonishment flood through him as he stared at the chief. "I'll be damned," he muttered. "Same song, different words."

3

Fargo saw Charlie Sycamore's face wrinkle in perplexity. "What are you saying, Fargo?" the man asked.

"Nothing. You wouldn't understand," Fargo said. "Where is his daughter?"

"Captured, taken by slave traders. They take her when Red Hawk is away and she is at lake," the scout said.

"You know these men?" Fargo questioned.

"I scout for Red Hawk. I ride, talk, listen, pay money. I learn name. Lucas DeLora. He is leader. He comes from Mexico."

"He's the one who's got her?"

Charlie Sycamore shrugged. "He runs slave trade. He takes girls to sell, special girls to special buyers for very much money. He meets buyers in Mexico. Some come from across ocean. That's all I hear. Beautiful, untouched daughter of a Kiowa chief would bring much money."

"Maybe not. She knows only Kiowan ways," Fargo said.

"She speaks the white man's tongue. Red Hawk had me teach her so she could talk to prisoners," the scout said.

"I didn't know you were this cozy with Red Hawk," Fargo said and the scout shrugged. "Maybe that's why General Stanford has never gotten to the Kiowa. Other tribes, but not the Kiowa." The mixed breed shrugged again, his face impassive. Fargo shifted his eyes to the chief. "Why doesn't the great chief go get his own daughter? Maybe he is not such a great chief, and his braves not such great warriors," he said.

Charlie Sycamore translated and Fargo saw the Indian's eyes flash, his voice tight as he answered the scout. "A great chief knows what he can and cannot do," Charlie Sycamore's voice came as he spoke for Red Hawk. "A great chief knows how his warriors can fight and how they cannot. For me to find my daughter I must track into towns where I could not go, speak to people who would not talk to me. My warriors and I would have to follow south, through Apache land, through Comanche land, across the land of the Mescalero, the Zuni, the Jicarilla. We would be attacked, again and again, on land we do not know. I cannot save my daughter if I am dead and my braves scattered to the winds."

"So you want me to do your job," Fargo said.

"You can go places that must be visited, speak to those who must be spoken to, find the trails that must be followed. Only you can find her and bring her back," Red Hawk said, his tone severe, no pleading in it. Something didn't fit. Fargo frowned. Red Hawk had to know it, too. Deciding to give voice to his thoughts, Fargo barked the question at the chief.

"I can say I will go, and once I'm away from here I can run," Fargo said.

"You will not do that. You are not the kind to do that," the Kiowa chief answered.

"You don't know that," Fargo protested.

"I know," Red Hawk said with complete certainty. Fargo frowned back. It still didn't fit. He let his glance scan the camp, where the others watched and waited. The odds were even worse, his chances to make a break nonexistent. But the thought of doing the Kiowa chief's bidding sickened him. Something good had to come out of it. Something positive had to be retrieved. He let his thoughts turn for another long moment.

"One way," he said. "I will look for her only one way. Red Hawk agrees to stop raiding and killing if I bring her back."

The chief fastened a glance of contempt at him when Charlie Sycamore had finished translating the demand. "No bargains," Red Hawk said. "No agreements. No promises. You will do what I tell you to do."

"Son of a bitch I will," Fargo said, his temper exploding at the Kiowa's unyielding arrogance. "Kill me—go ahead. That won't get your daughter back." It was a dangerous challenge, but he had no other choice. Fargo swore inwardly.

Red Hawk motioned to Charlie Sycamore and barked an order to his braves. "Bring him," he said and strode toward the dense green wall of trees at the end of the camp. Six braves instantly surrounded Fargo and he was pushed forward in the chief's footsteps. He'd gone some twenty yards, he guessed, when the thick trees opened up on a cleared area. Four Conestogas were there, in a semicircle, and beside them were some thirty men, women, and children guarded by fifteen Kiowa braves. Some of the men wore bandages and bruises, as did a few of the women. He saw that the children ranged from toddlers to those in their early teens. All stared at Fargo with eyes so filled with fear and despair that hope dared not flicker.

Red Hawk turned to Fargo, icy contempt in his voice. "They all die unless you go after my daughter. They die, one by one, unless you bring her back," he said.

Fargo cursed silently. He had learned why the Kiowa chief knew he would not flee. His eyes moved across the faces of the captives. He knew he would obey Red Hawk's orders, and again cursed the cunning of the man. But he remained silent, unwilling to give the Indian his devil's victory too quickly. Red Hawk raised his arm again. "There is more," he said, and Charlie Sycamore clapped his hands together. The thick foliage parted and Fargo saw the flash of the corn-silk hair first, then the slender figure being pushed into the clearing.

Jessica Winter met his stare and he saw the regret in her eyes as she half shrugged. "How the hell did you get here?" Fargo hissed at her.

"I rode this way. I was going to wait for you and try to talk to you again away from the camp," Jessica said. "Suddenly I was surrounded. I guess they were waiting for you, too."

"You guess right, and this could be your last right guess," Fargo rasped. His eyes went to the hostages beside the wagons, and he swore again at the Kiowa chief. The man would not hesitate to kill each and every one of his captives. Fargo's eyes returned to Jessica. Despite the fear he knew she felt, she stood with her back stiff and straight. It was a strength, he realized, and she'd need every bit of it. But he felt the thoughts inside him crackling, beginning to form themselves as his eyes passed over the hostages again, lingering on their children. Most were too young to realize how little hope was left for them.

He was trapped, Fargo knew. He'd have to try and find Red Hawk's daughter. He'd have to do the cunning, ruthless murdering man's bidding as if he were a friend, trying with every bit of skill and trail wisdom inside him. It was the only chance any of these poor people had to stay alive. Once again he brought his eyes back to Jessica. To do what he had to do he'd need help. There was no way to know what he'd run into. Another pair of eyes, another pair of hands, a messenger or a decoy or a lookout, whatever was needed, he thought to himself. But it had to be someone he could trust, someone with the strength to stay and the heart to commit.

She'd have to do, Fargo told himself. Besides, he had no one else, he thought with his ever-present practical realism. He fastened Jessica with a long glance, and her eyes were steady as they met his gaze. "I'm going to save your ass, but I want your word on something," he said.

"Yes, of course," Jessica said.

"I get you out of this and you're going to help me save these people," Fargo told her.

"Yes, you have my word. I want to see them saved, too," Jessica said.

"You're going to follow my orders, whatever, whenever, wherever, understand?" She nodded vigorously. Fargo turned to Charlie Sycamore. "Tell him she goes with me or I don't go," Fargo said, and the scout quickly translated. The chief agreed without hesitation, and Fargo felt a stab of instant uneasiness he wished he could explain. But he couldn't and flung the moment aside. "The girl has a name. What is it?" Fargo questioned.

Charlie Sycamore answered at once. "Moonrise. She is called Moonrise," he said. Fargo nodded and Red Hawk barked a command. In moments, two braves appeared, one leading the Ovaro, the other Jessica's tan gelding. The Kiowa chief turned to Fargo, his stern face unchanged, made of imperious confidence, his voice a thing of deadly softness. From someone else it might have seemed a plea, but from the Kiowa chief it was a deadly promise.

"Bring her back, Trailsman. It is all in your hands now. Everything. Everyone." He turned on his heel and strode away, disappearing into the wall of trees. The others silently followed. All but the black-clad figure of Charlie

44

Sycamore. He stayed, watching, as Jessica pulled herself onto the tan gelding.

"Don't try to follow me, Charlie," Fargo said. "I don't want anyone looking over my shoulder."

"What if I do, Fargo?" the man returned.

"I'll kill you," Fargo said very softly. "Count on it." He climbed onto the Ovaro and moved the horse forward at a walk. Jessica swung in beside him as he rode to the edge of the stream and glanced back at the Kiowa camp before turning south. He felt Jessica's eyes studying him and glanced back at her.

"Say it, whatever's poking at you," he tossed at her.

"Would you really shoot a man for following you?" she asked.

"Some men," he said.

"And Charlie Sycamore's one of them?" she queried.

"That's right. Red Hawk calls the tune with him. That's pretty plain now, but that wouldn't stop Charlie from working his own deals if he got the chance. I'm not about to give him that chance," Fargo said.

"It's still all so barbaric," she said, disapproval in her tone.

"Maybe so, but I've never had much success in talking a rattlesnake out of his striking," Fargo said and put the pinto into a trot. Jessica moved up to stay at his side. He noted the dust sliding over the land. When he found a stand of red cedar and a half-circle of good downy bromegrass, he pulled to a halt. "We bed down here," he said, sliding from his horse. "You have your own rations?"

"Yes," she said. "But not all that much. We'll have to stop somewhere and get more." He nodded as he unsaddled the Ovaro. Jessica took the gear from the gelding and settled down beside him as the night fell and a half-moon rose in the black velvet sky. Her corn-silk hair shimmered with a pale glow in the moonlight. He watched her eat a strip of dried beef from her saddlebag. "I can't just forget why I came here," Jessica reminded him. "I still want to find my uncle. Do you think he could have been caught by Red Hawk, the way that wagon train was?"

"Red Hawk, or maybe the Kansa or the Pawnee. The Kiowa aren't the only ones that ride this land. We can ask about him while we're tracking for Moonrise, but don't get any hopes up," Fargo said.

"Hope is all I've left," she said.

"What did he look like?"

"Ted Winter cared about people and it showed in his face. He had kind, patient eyes," Jessica began.

"Don't tell me what showed in his face," Fargo interrupted, more harshly than he'd intended, and saw her lips tighten at once. "Not many people we meet are going to know what kind eyes are. Give me something I can use."

"He was tall, taller than you, and very thin, with a lot of silver hair. He also had a slight limp from an accident when he was a boy," she said.

"That's better," Fargo said. "Now I'm going to get some sleep and I suggest you do the same. We'll be riding hard tomorrow."

"Yes, I am tired," she said, rose, and went to her saddlebag to get her things. As she stepped into the trees, Fargo shed all but his undershorts, laid the Colt in its holster alongside him, and stretched out on a blanket. Jessica returned in moments, a sheet wrapped around her, which she used as a combination coat and blanket. She lay down wrapped in the sheet, and he saw her eyes move across his muscled smoothness. "You going to sleep that way?" she asked.

"What way?"

"Uncovered. Almost naked," she said.

"The night's still hot. You bothered?" he answered.

"I just don't approve of displaying oneself," she said stiffly.

"That's too bad," Fargo said evenly. Her eyes stayed on him, waiting, and she raised herself on one elbow.

"Well?" she asked. "Is that all you have to say?"

"Turn over," he said.

The dark blue eyes glared back. "I shall do precisely that," she said, and he smiled inwardly at how long it took for her to turn her back to him. But finally he heard the sound of her breathing grow deep with sleep, and he closed his eyes and let the night wrap itself around him.

He woke with the new sun's first rays and looked across at her. One beautifully long leg stuck out from inside the sheet, the thigh slender but not thin and the calf a long curve. He rose and she stirred, lifting a nicely molded knee. He pulled on jeans and his gun belt and stepped to the edge of the trees. Turning as he heard her sit up, he saw her shake the shock of corn-silk hair and rub sleep from her eyes as she pushed to her feet. She caught the top edge of the sheet as it fell away to reveal the long curve of one breast.

"Get dressed. There's water nearby," he said.

"Someplace you know?" she asked.

"No, but it's there," he said.

"What makes you so sure?" she asked, and he gestured to a flight of redwings, tree swallows, and meadowlarks.

"Birds fly to water in the morning, away from it in the evening," he said. She rose, wrapped the sheet around herself, and disappeared into the trees. She returned dressed in a brown skirt and tan shirt, the top clinging to the long curve of her breasts as she combed the corn-silk hair, looking aristocratically beautiful. The morning sun was already burning, so he kept his shirt off as he saddled the pinto and swung onto the horse. Jessica saddled up and came alongside him as he followed the songbirds in the sky. He soon came upon a small lake, hardly more than a pond, set in a rock-bound circle that was itself surrounded by box elder. "Enjoy it. There won't be many more where we're going," Fargo told her.

"I'm not going to put on an exhibition for you," Jessica said. "I expect you'll be a gentleman and promise not to watch."

"You expect wrong, but this is your lucky day. I'm not going to be around to watch," Fargo said.

"You're going to leave me here alone?" Jessica asked, alarm instant in her voice.

"You can't have it both ways," Fargo said and saw consternation join the alarm in her face. "I'm not going to be that far away," he laughed. "Anything happens, you scream and I'll hear you. By the time you've had your bath and dried off, I'll be back. Take your time. Enjoy yourself."

"All right," she said, slid from her horse, and started toward the pond, moving through the passages between the rocks that led down to the edge of the water. Fargo turned the Ovaro back into the box elder that surrounded the rocks. He walked the horse into the trees and halted where he could see out to the edge of the tree line where it met the rocks. Sitting quietly as a toad on a lily pad, he let his gaze move slowly across the edge of the trees, scanning back and forth, watching every little movement of leaf and branch. Almost an hour had gone by when he saw the covey of harlequin quail suddenly take flight. Leaning forward in the saddle, he saw the black-clad figure crawling onto one of the rocks to peer down at the pond.

Fargo let a long sigh escape him as he moved the Ovaro forward. Once again, as he had so often in the past, he realized that being right did not always bring pleasure. He stayed inside the trees as he circled the rocks, finally halting again, swinging from the horse this time to step into the open only a dozen feet from the figure on its stomach peering down at the pond. "Why didn't you listen to me, Charlie?" he asked, his voice soft, almost tired.

Charlie Sycamore stiffened, slid backward from the rock, and found his feet as he turned to face Fargo. His eyes were narrow, opaque blue slits. "Tell me one thing. Red Hawk tell you to follow me?" Fargo questioned.

"No," the scout said.

"Didn't think so," Fargo answered. "I told you what I'd do if you came after me."

The thin, angular face remained expressionless, but Fargo saw Charlie Sycamore's fingers rub against each other. It was the only tiny indication of the man's sudden nervousness. "Everybody makes mistakes," the scout said. "Guess I made one."

"You did," Fargo said. He swore at himself and let another sigh escape him. "I must be getting soft. The girl said it'd be barbaric to shoot you just for following. I'm going to listen to her."

"Tell her thanks," Charlie Sycamore said.

"Next time I won't even call your name," Fargo said and received a nod. "Now drop your gun and leave your horse. You're walking."

He saw the man's eyes widen, sudden fear in their blue depths. "No, I ride. I must ride," Charlie Sycamore said. "I need horse."

Fargo frowned back. "No horse," he said.

"I must have horse," the man insisted.

"You've got no choice, mister. Don't press me. I could change my mind," Fargo said, his voice hardening. He felt the surprise go through him as Charlie Sycamore's hand darted down to his holster. The scout was fast, Fargo saw, faster than he'd expected. But not that fast, as with the speed of a rattler's strike, Fargo's hand slapped the edge of his holster and the Colt seemed to leap into his hand. The revolver barked, a single shot, just as Charlie Sycamore brought his gun hand up with his own gun in it. Fargo's shot slammed into the scout's chest and the man flew backward as though he'd been kicked by a mule, a stream of red spurting from him. Charlie Sycamore's gun went off as his finger tightened on the trigger in an automatic reflex, the shot hitting the trunk of a tree. The man's body shuddered once as he lay on his back and was still.

"Damn," Fargo said, pulling his lips back as he stared down at the lifeless figure of Charlie Sycamore. "You should've quit while you were ahead," he murmured and strode back to the Ovaro. He swung onto the horse, and the frown stayed on his brow as he rode downward through the rocks toward the pond. Charlie Sycamore had lied about Red Hawk to him. That had become clear. Charlie knew how fast he was with a six-gun, yet he'd elected to draw on him rather than not have his horse. Only one thing was important enough to make him do that. He'd been more afraid of being caught by Red Hawk. He needed the horse to run fast and far, which meant the Kiowa chief had sent him to follow after them.

They'd both lost now, master and servant, Fargo thought. Now the Kiowa chief would have to wait without reports— and that was good, Fargo reflected. He'd dare not take any actions against his hostages because he was dissatisfied. He'd dare not give in to impatience. The hostages had just won a little more time, even though they wouldn't know it. But the final day would come, Fargo knew, and Red Hawk would be waiting. The one and only hope remained unchanged. He had to find Moonrise. Fargo threaded between two rocks to see Jessica, dressed, a towel in one hand, watching as he approached, her dark blue eyes questioning.

"Charlie Sycamore?" she breathed. "And you killed him, just as you said you would," she added, the disapproval plain in her voice.

"Not just as I said I would. I listened to you," Fargo said. "I was going to let him have one mistake. He made two."

"You went out expecting he'd be following," she accused.

"I had to be sure."

"And you knew he'd watch me in the pond."

"Does a fox watch a henhouse?" Fargo asked, dismounted, and started toward the pond. "Now I'm going to wash off whatever will come off," he said and began to shed clothes and gun belt as he reached the edge of the water.

"I'll wait up here," Jessica called out primly, her tone telling him she'd not watch.

"You do whatever you like, honey," Fargo said as he stepped naked into the water and let the coolness wash over him. He swam, washed, turned lazily in the clear water, and was willing to wager that Jessica was not looking away, not entirely. He let himself enjoy the moment, until finally he rose and lay down on one of the rocks to let the burning sun dry him off. A towel dropped down from the rocks to land half across one leg, and he sat up and began to dry himself. The smile stayed with him as he finished, dressed, and climbed up through the passage. She turned as he came up to her with the towel. "Thought you weren't going to watch?" he slid at her.

"I didn't," she said. "I heard you come out of the water and just threw the towel."

"Didn't your mother tell you it's not nice to lie?" He

laughed as he tossed the towel to her and walked to the pinto.

"Don't judge everyone by your lack of good behavior," she returned as she hurried to the gelding. He led the way from the pond at a walk, headed down across the slowly sloping land, and rode south again. By early afternoon the land had changed its face, quickly taking on the characteristics of the southwest territory, stretching out with long expanses of gray-green creosote bush and low hillsides of rock, paloverde trees, and honey mesquite.

The land became dry, harsh, with only trickles of water sliding along rock crevices. When they came onto a small rock pool, he halted to let the horses drink and to refill their canteens. A faint layer of perspiration made Jessica's tan shirt cling to her, outlining the curve of her breasts and the tiny points that tipped the full undersides. "Where do you start to look?" she asked, a hint of despair in her voice. "It seems impossible, like hunting for a needle in a haystack."

"There's a town some miles on. We can reach it before dark. We'll start there," Fargo said.

"You think slave traders would stop in a town?" Jessica asked.

"They'll need supplies just as anybody else would, maybe fresh horses, maybe a wagon repaired. It's a long, hard haul into Mexico," Fargo said. "You see, you have the wrong idea about these men. You think they'll be sneaking around, hiding the girls they have. They'll be damn protective about them, but they won't be hiding them. Nobody down here's going to blink an eye about the slave trade."

"My God, how disgusting," Jessica said.

"Maybe so, but that's the way it is, and in this case, be glad for it. It'll work in our favor. We'll have a chance to pick up a trail," Fargo said.

"I can't be glad for anything concerning men such as

those," Jessica said. "Not even the chance to pick up a trail. You'll find another way, some other tracks."

"Keep hoping," Fargo said as he guided the way up the side of a slope. Jessica paused to admire the pink-red blossoms of a golden hedgehog cactus.

"How lovely," she said. "Beauty comes at you suddenly out here, doesn't it?"

"Everything comes at you suddenly out here, even the things you'd expect to just pass by. You've got to know this land to survive in it. It keeps its secret places very well hidden. That's why the Comanche and the Apache can fight and survive where others can't. They're part of this land. Red Hawk was smart enough to know that. He knew he couldn't sneak his way, talk his way, or fight his way."

"What makes you think we can?" Jessica asked. "Do you know the land like the Apache?"

"Nobody knows it like the Apache or the Comanche. But I've been through it more than the Kiowa. We'll see what I can find," Fargo said, reaching a low rise and pointing through the gathering dusk to where a collection of houses took shape. "Chulu," he said.

"Chulu?" she repeated. "What's it mean?"

"It's the Mexican name for the coatimundi," Fargo said. "It gets more traffic than most towns in the territory—travelers on their way south to the border, north to the *cimarrón* cutoff, or west to nowhere."

"Then they probably have a hotel. I'd like a good night's sleep in a proper bed. God knows how long before I get another one," Jessica said.

"God knows," Fargo agreed and put the pinto into a trot. The buildings grew larger and twilight arrived in town just as they did. Fargo slowed as he led the way down the wide expanse of the main street, which was unpaved and dry with little whorls of dust stirred up by a steady stream of heavy-wheeled Texas wagons, battered Conestogas, converted Owensboro huckster wagons, and one-horse spring wagons with extra-heavy undergear. Fargo drew to a halt outside a peeling structure that bore a sign: BED & BOARD. Dismounting, he went inside with Jessica. A middle-aged bald man in shirtsleeves and vest greeted them.

"I'd like a room for the night," Jessica said and threw Fargo a quick glance.

"Why not?" he half shrugged. "Make it two. Next to each other."

"There's a public stable down the street," the man said as he pushed the register at them. Jessica signed in first, then Fargo put his name under hers. The man handed each a large key.

"Six and seven, down the hall," he said.

"Anyplace to eat around here?" Jessica asked.

"We serve till eight. Nothing fancy, though," the clerk said.

"It'll be fine, whatever it is," Jessica said and followed Fargo outside and to the stable. He unsaddled, turned the Ovaro over to a stable man, and walked out with Jessica as she carried her travel bag.

"Sleep well," he said.

"You're not eating with me?" She frowned.

"I'll get something at the saloon. I'll be asking questions. There's no better place for it. I'll see you in the morning," he said.

"All right," Jessica said and trudged away with her traveling bag. The night had descended, and Fargo walked through the dark street to the square oasis of yellow light and noise that unquestionably marked the town saloon. He entered a very ordinary saloon with the usual long bar at one side and a dozen round tables spread across a sawdust-covered floor. The place was already crowded, with customers at the tables and the bar, most of them men in work clothes, a few wearing the outfits of drummers or snake-oil sellers. Fargo found a spot at the bar and waited for the bartender, a portly figure with a red-cheeked, beefy face, short, graying hair, and weary eyes.

"Bourbon. No watered-down whiskey," Fargo said and instantly drew a modicum of respect from the barkeep and was served a measure of reasonably good whiskey. Fargo sipped the drink, ordered a venison sandwich, and listened to the bar talk that was boringly similar to all bar talk, made of wild stories, booze-filled exaggerations, and coarse jokes. When he finished his sandwich he struck up a conversation with some of the customers nearby and knew the bartender was listening with one ear. "I'm looking for a man name of Lucas DeLora. Anybody here know him?" Fargo asked casually.

"Lucas DeLora?" a man echoed. "Nope, don't know him."

"A lot of people don't give their names," Fargo said. "He's a slave trader. He had an Indian girl with him."

"Indian girl?" another man said. "No, didn't see anybody with an Indian girl."

"He could've had her outside in a wagon," Fargo said.

"Didn't see any squaw in a wagon," the man said as others set down their glasses and moved in closer behind him. One, a big, thick-lipped man with beetle brows, leaned forward.

"Who're you, mister? You a lawman?" he queried.

"No. The name's Fargo," Skye said, keeping his voice casual.

"What do you care about some Comanche bitch?" the thick-lipped one pressed.

"She's not Comanche. She's Kiowa," Fargo corrected.

55

"Same thing. She's an Indian. Why all the interest in her?" the man persisted.

"Been asked to find her," Fargo said and heard the low murmur of the crowd.

"Why?" someone else asked.

"To get her away from that slave trader," Fargo said.

"Why? You a goddamn Indian-lover?" the thick-lipped man put in, growing more belligerent and infecting the others with his attitude.

"No. I'm just doing a job," Fargo said.

"You being paid to save some Kiowa bitch?" one of the others queried, and an angry murmur followed at once.

"Not paid, but it's something I've got to do," Fargo said.

"Because you want to. You're a goddamn Indian-lover, that's what," the beetle-browed one snapped back. "You know what we do to Indian-lovers around here?" He started forward, others with him, some ten at least, and Fargo took a step back from the bar to face them.

"Let's show him," someone called out, and Fargo swore inwardly. Suddenly it was all out of hand, all the ugliness of hate erupting, mindless venom sweeping across the room, instant, explosive proof that the worst of human behavior was too easily set loose. They came at him, the thick-lipped one leading.

"You ever been tarred and feathered, Fargo? You ain't gonna enjoy it," he snarled.

"You ever get a bullet in the gut, mister? You won't be enjoying that, either," Fargo said as he backed away. He flung a glance at the bartender in hopes—as barkeeps often did—he'd try to keep order. This one merely looked on as the heavy man in the forefront kept coming, others pushing him. He had gone too far to back down, and Fargo knew there was little choice left. The men suddenly surged, began to rush him, and he drew the big Colt, lowered it a fraction, and fired. "Ow, Jesus," the heavy one screamed as his kneecap shattered and he fell. The others paused, but gripped in their collective rage, Fargo saw them start to draw their own six-guns as they started forward again.

He fired twice more, not lowering the gun this time, and two of the men fell as he dived to the floor, rolling, and heard the explosion of shots that hurled past him. He came up behind a table, upending it as he did, diving behind it and firing off another shot that spun one of the attackers around before he fell. Half running, half tumbling, yanking the table along on its side as two bullets thudded into it, he reached the door and dived through it as another hail of bullets slammed into the door frame. Outside, he somersaulted, came up on one knee, and was facing the saloon doors as the crowd burst out. He fired off two more shots and two of the attackers fell. The rest drew back for a moment and Fargo was on his feet, streaking through the darkness.

He heard the others bursting out of the saloon again, shouting curses, and he darted down a narrow alleyway between two warehouse buildings. He dropped to one knee, paused and reloaded and listened to the men scatter to search for him, joined by others from inside the saloon. They were running through the street, searching aimlessly yet cautiously, unwilling to be ambushed. They'd stop that soon enough and begin to search with a proper pattern. "Four of you get back to the hitching post," Fargo heard one call out, and his lips thinned. They'd begun to control their searching. He was a stranger in town and he had to have ridden in. When he didn't return to the hitching post to try and retrieve his horse, they'd figure out he had stabled his mount.

Fargo rose and ran silently down the alleyway to the back of the buildings. He guessed they'd be another five or six minutes searching, then another three deciding his horse wasn't at the hitching post outside the bar. That gave him damn little time to do what he had to do, but it'd have to be enough. He ran along the back of the buildings, passed the bar, halted and dropped on one knee in a stretch of deep shadow as three searchers ran out in front of him, searching past a cluster of buildings off the main street. They went by and he ran forward again, reached the inn, and raced past the desk clerk and down the corridor. He paused at the first of the two rooms, drew his foot back, and kicked the flimsy lock open, then plunged inside.

He was at the bed, his hand over Jessica's mouth as she sat up, her eyes wide with surprise and fright. "It's me," he hissed. "Get dressed." He took his hand from her face and stepped back as she swung herself from the bed. The dim light from the lone window showed she wore a thin pink nightgown that outlined the curves of her long breasts.

"I'm not dressing with you standing there," she said, pulling a bedsheet half over herself.

"Goddammit," he swore and strode to the doorway, where he peered into the corridor, his back to her and the Colt in his hand.

"What's all this about?" she asked as she dressed.

"I'll explain later. Hurry up, damn it," he called back. It seemed an endless moment, but he knew it was but minutes before Jessica came to him, the traveling bag slung over one shoulder. He led the way down the corridor. "You go to the stable and get the horses. If the stable boy gives you any problem, tell him you'll shoot him," Fargo said, and she frowned at him. "Just do it. Tell him to help you saddle the horses," Fargo said. "There's a rear door, I saw it. When you hear shots, you ride out the rear door."

"Where will you be?"

"Waiting, I hope," he said, and Jessica strode from the

hotel. He stayed inside, watched her hurry down the street, and turned at the desk clerk's voice.

"What's going on, mister?" the man asked.

"Nothing that concerns you," Fargo said.

"I don't want trouble here," the clerk muttered.

"You won't get any, 'less you make it," Fargo said and backed from the doorway as he saw three figures spread out as they searched among the buildings. They saw Jessica heading for the stable, but they'd no reason to connect her with him and went their way down alleyways between structures. Fargo went into a crouch as he slipped from the doorway into the night, pressing himself against the side of the hotel as he moved forward. Jessica had reached the stable, he was certain. He saw another four figures coming down the main street. He stayed in the crouch as he hurried to the rear corner of the hotel and darted across the open space toward the stable, grateful for the dark.

The four figures had reached the hotel and were on their way to the stable. Fargo dropped to one knee beside a corner of the stable as he cursed softly. Jessica would need another two minutes to get both horses saddled, but he didn't have two minutes more. He raised the Colt, took aim at the nearest of the four men. Jessica would hear the shots and realize they were the signal for her to race out the rear door of the stable. Only she wouldn't be ready to go. He cursed again as he wondered if she'd freeze in indecision or panic and try to hide inside the stable. Either one would end any chance of escape. But he had no choice, he realized. The men were only steps from the stable, and others were coming down the street after them.

Fargo fired two shots, and two of the figures toppled as though they were ninepins in a bowling alley. The rest broke and dived for cover, self-protection their first reaction. Fargo fired off another shot without waiting to aim as he raced down the side of the stable. He'd bought at least forty-five seconds, as they'd pause before rushing into the stable, uncertain exactly where the shots had come from. He ran in a crouch, reached the rear of the stable as the doors flew open and Jessica came out on the gelding, leading the Ovaro behind. Fargo straightened up, dug heels into the ground, and streaked for the horses. Jessica was clinging tightly to the gelding, he noted as he neared.

"The cinch isn't tightened. Didn't have time," she shouted and steered toward him. He nodded as he came alongside and leaped, grabbed a handful of the black mane and swung himself onto the Ovaro's broad back. He felt the saddle slip at once and tightened his thighs as he clung to the horse and Jessica tossed him the reins. Shouts and a half-dozen wild shots came from behind, and Fargo swung to the right, Jessica coming in beside him. "They coming after us? We'll have to stop and tighten the cinches to make time," Jessica shouted.

"No, they'd have to go back and get their horses and they won't go to all that bother," Fargo said, slowed the Ovaro, and pulled to a halt inside a cluster of paloverde. He swung to the ground and began to tighten the cinch around the Ovaro's midsection as Jessica did the same with the gelding.

"I'd just put the saddles on when I heard the shots," Jessica said. "I thought I'd best go, cinch or no cinch."

"You did right," Fargo said, tightening the strap under the horse's body and swinging back into the saddle.

"What happened?" Jessica asked, coming alongside him as he moved out of the trees.

"It all went wrong," he said.

"You find out anything?" she queried.

"Yes. It's not a friendly town and they don't like Indians," he said grimly.

"Now what?" Jessica asked.

"We find another town," he said. "But first we find a spot to bed down." He led the way down an incline. The moon was in the midnight sky when he halted at a spot mostly made of low rock and dense growths of jojoba shrubs, plenty thick enough to sleep in out of sight. He put the horses behind the rocks and dropped a blanket in the shrubs. Jessica had picked out a spot nearby. He saw only the pale gleam of her hair as she sat up.

"So much for a good night's sleep in a proper bed," she said.

"Next time, maybe," he said as he lay down and watched a great horned owl watching him.

"You mishandled it back there, didn't you?" Jessica asked tartly from where she lay.

"I didn't mishandle it," he answered and heard the irritation in his voice. "I just didn't expect they'd be so damn prickly about Indians."

"You mishandled it," she said almost smugly. He wanted to snap back at her but stayed silent, aware that while she wasn't right, she wasn't entirely wrong, either. "Maybe you'd best let me try next time," Jessica's voice came.

"Go to sleep," he growled, knowing the suggestion would come up again. He closed his eyes and slept.

4

The morning sun rose to quickly bake the land. Fargo used a little of the water in his canteen to drink and wash. When he was dressed, he walked behind the rocks and gave half the water left in the canteen to the Ovaro. Leading both horses back with him, he heard Jessica inside the thick jojoba. When she stood up, he saw the yellow corn-silk hair had been pulled back and held in place by a tortoiseshell clip. With her hair pulled back, the gracefulness of her neck was apparent. She came toward him, shirtsleeves rolled up. A green cotton skirt with a slit gave her slender figure freedom of movement.

"We need to find water," she said, holding up her canteen. He held out one hand and she gave him the container. Hefting it, he felt that it was more than half empty. Unscrewing the lid, he held it up for the gelding to drink. "What are you doing? That's all I have," Jessica protested.

"You'll wait till we find some more," Fargo said. "In this country, watering your horse is the most important thing—'less you want to die walking. Then you drink, and only a little. You drank damn near the whole canteen."

Jessica peered across the hot, arid terrain. "You know where we can find more water?" she asked.

"No, but we'll find it in time," he said and swung onto the pinto. "Let's ride."

"Just wandering?"

"There's an outfit due south. I was there once, man named Carronna runs it. He fixes old wagons, sells them, and runs a way station. He also sells water from a well he owns," Fargo said. "It's a place Lucas DeLora would visit and one we have to visit." He moved the Ovaro at a walk. Jessica rode beside him and watched as his eyes swept the rugged slopes that rose up on all sides of the alluvial plain where they rode.

"You looking for signs of water?" she asked.

"I'm looking for signs of Apache," Fargo said and saw the instant fright touch her face as she followed his gaze. But he saw no quick movements, no waiting figures as he moved to ride closer to the bottom of the rugged slopes. Their rocky fastness glowered down on the two intruders, their austere grayness broken by sudden appearances of a juniper tree or a deep green, starburst-shaped sotal plant.

An occasional bighorn sheep moved into view and just as suddenly bounded away. Three feral burros ambled along a rock ridge and vanished. It was not only a harsh landscape but a silent one, where creatures seemed to move soundlessly. When the walls of a wash descended downward, Fargo followed. At the bottom he moved across a sunken plain that was a carpet of interwoven greens—the gray-green of creosote bushes, the pale yellow of the paloverde trees, and the dark green of mesquite. The sun had crossed the burning sky into afternoon when Jessica drew to a halt. "Can we rest some? My throat's so dry I can hardly swallow," she said.

He dismounted and held his canteen out to her. "Three swallows," he said.

"Three swallows?" she echoed, protest in her voice, but she held the canteen to her lips and obeyed. When she finished, he took a swallow and gave some more of the water

63

to the Ovaro and the tan gelding. He climbed back onto the pinto and moved forward.

"Keep riding," he said. The long, sunken plain began to rise slowly, the long wash coming to an end, and Fargo saw a dome-shaped tall hill rise, a passageway leading upward. It was studded with growths of bristlebrush, but more importantly, he spotted woolly lifferns and a coating of green algae on the rocks. He increased the pinto's pace as the horse climbed the passage.

"What is it?" Jessica called out.

"A *tinaja*," Fargo said as she followed close behind.

"What's that?" she asked.

"A natural water basin in a rock crater," he said, rounded a curve in the passage, and reined up as the lava basin lay directly in front of him, more than half filled with water. Jessica dismounted at once and rushed to the sloping side of the basin, taking her canteen with her.

"Is it fed by an underground spring?" she asked.

"No. *Tinajas* get their water strictly from rain," Fargo said, and she frowned back.

"But there's hardly any rain here," she said. "Not in this land."

"That's right, but because the basins are solid lava rock, the water that falls into them is not absorbed into the ground," he explained as he knelt down beside her to fill his canteen. When he finished, he filled his hat with the water and let each horse drink. The burning sun had started to sink beneath the dome of the high hills, and Jessica sat with her back against a rock. Her shirt, wet with perspiration, clung to her, revealing the line of her breasts and the tiny points on each, almost as though she wore nothing. She saw his eyes enjoying the sight and sat up straight, pulling the shirt from her body and tossing a glance of disapproval at him.

"We'll stay in these hills till it gets dark, another hour or so, I'd guess," he said and climbed onto the Ovaro. Jessica rode beside him as he threaded the way through rock passages where the lava formations grew taller and the algae disappeared from the rock surfaces as they left the *tinaja*.

They had gone another half hour when he yanked the pinto to a halt and put one finger to his lips. Jessica's eyes followed his gaze and she saw the half-dozen horsemen moving along a stone rise toward them. Fargo cursed softly as he took in the bandannas they wore on their foreheads, the lithe but smallish half-naked figures, faces without the broad-cheeked strength of the northern plains red man, black hair hanging long, most wearing long loincloths, feet clothed in army boots.

"Apache. They haven't seen us yet," he whispered and backed the Ovaro into a passage between high rocks. Jessica followed behind him as he led the way through the rocks, saw another cut and turned into it, pulling to a halt to listen. His lips drew back in a grimace as he heard the sound of the Apache as they grunted short, terse exchanges. "They know we're here, damn it," he said.

"How?" Jessica breathed.

"They heard us, smelled us, or sensed us. They'll be searching," Fargo said and sent the Ovaro through a narrower cut in the walls of high rock. The cut led upward and twisted. He heard the sounds of the Apache ponies behind as they picked up speed. They were beginning to file out through the passages. Fargo saw the cut he was in end at a steep slope of high rock. The mouth of a cave rose up in front of him, and he motioned to Jessica as he dismounted and led the way into the cavern. The odor caught at his nostrils at once, dank and musty and something else, a strange sweet-sour quality to it.

The cavern was tall and deep, and he moved further into

its rock walls as the light quickly began to grow dim. The cavern stayed tall but narrowed some as he continued deeper. The dimness deepened and soon edged toward total blackness. Fargo halted, unwilling to go further into stygian gloom. He turned and Jessica was there, dimly visible. The sweet-sour odor had grown stronger and the mouth of the cavern was only a tiny pinpoint of light now.

He faced the distant cave entrance, dropped to one knee, and drew the big Henry from its saddle case. "You think they'll come in here?" Jessica breathed.

"They'll give a look. I'm hoping they won't come in this far," he said. "But I want to be ready if they do."

"What's that strange odor?" Jessica said, and he saw her eyes travel upward to the ceiling of the cave. She stared for a moment, her eyes moving across the top of the cave, and he saw her lips come open and her eyes suddenly grow wide. "Oh, God. Oh, my God," she whispered as she became aware of the black shapes hanging from the cavern ceiling, heads down, wings folded against their bodies. "Bats, thousands of them," she breathed, and he felt her hand dig into his arm.

"They won't be bothering you," Fargo said. "Not for now."

"What does that mean?" she asked, her eyes still on the densely packed shapes that covered the ceiling of the cave.

"It means they'll stay right where they are until night falls," he said.

"That'll be damn soon," Jessica said, an edge of panic coming into her voice.

"It's not here yet," Fargo said. And then, his voice hardening, he ordered, "Be quiet." She fell silent with a sharp intake of breath. Fargo raised the big rifle as he heard the voices at the mouth of the cavern. He let ears more than eyes follow the movements of the Apache, two or three of them, he guessed, inside the cave now, pushing forward cautiously. They moved slowly, halted, and listened as they peered into the black recesses of the cavern. Fargo prayed the horses wouldn't blow air. His finger rested on the trigger of the rifle, his breath but a tiny stream of air between his lips. But he heard the soft shuffling sound. They were backing out. He waited another long minute before lowering the rifle and drawing a deep breath.

"Can we get out of here now?" Jessica asked.

"No," he said.

"No?" she echoed and cast a glance at the bats.

"They backed out because they couldn't see back here. The Apache won't walk into a trap or be ambushed. It's their nature to be careful. But they'll wait outside when they don't find us anywhere else," Fargo said.

"For how long?" Jessica asked.

"Till they're convinced we're not in here," he said, sidestepping the question inside the question. He shifted position and leaned against the nearest wall. Jessica rested on her knees beside him. The cavern grew darker and Fargo saw the gray light from the entrance quickly fading. The night would be on them soon. As if in agreement, he heard the rustling sound, a scraping fluttering, thousands of wings moving, rubbing together and against each other as they began to stir.

"Oh, God," Jessica breathed. "We've got to get out of here."

"Not till it's dark," Fargo said. "They've got at least one sentry waiting."

Jessica's eyes went to the blackness of the cave ceiling. "I can't stay in here when they start flying. I can't," she murmured.

Fargo lay the rifle against his leg. He'd hold her down and gag her with his hand, he was deciding. Then the sound of the wings grew louder and another sound came—the horses moving nervously. He swore silently. The horses would surely spook when the thousands of bats took flight in the confined quarters of the cavern. He swore again. He could hold Jessica and keep her silent, but not the horses. When they whinnied in panic, any Apache outside would hear them. Fargo picked up the rifle again and rose to one knee. "Take hold of your horse," he whispered. "When I start, you go with me and hit the saddle when we reach the entrance. Understand?" She nodded and he swore inwardly again. The horses, senses on edge, were fidgeting. There was no choice. They had to make a break for it, using the swarming bats as a cover.

The scraping of thousands of wings increased again, along with the flapping and now the shrill, squeaking noise. With their built-in alarm clocks, the long-nosed bats responded to the call of the night. With a rush of whooshing, swishing sound, split with shrill cries, they burst into flight, filling the cavern with winged bodies. Fargo felt a dozen hit against him as they swooped around, over and under any obstacle in their way. The Ovaro surged forward, snorting, and Fargo ran with the reins in hand. "Oh, God, oh, God," he heard Jessica cry out as she ran with the gelding. The cavern was blackness filled with swooping, crashing bodies in flight from wall to wall and ceiling to floor. Eyes half-closed, Fargo ran through and with the swarm of bats, yanking on the reins as he realized the horse was near panic.

He felt more than saw the gelding draw alongside him with Jessica, who half gasped, half screamed as she ran. The cave entrance loomed up, a dark shape just ahead, almost obscured by the curtain of bats. "Now," he shouted as he pulled himself up onto the Ovaro, clinging to the horse's back, flattening himself so they could clear the entrance ceiling. He glimpsed Jessica on the gelding a half-length behind him as he raced from the cave, the torrent of bats preceding both horses. He also heard the shouts of two Apache, perhaps three, then the explosion of rifle fire. But they were shooting wildly, unable to get a clear shot through the curtain of bats that were one upon the other, a wall of winged bodies. He spied the narrow cut to his right and sent the Ovaro into it, racing forward as the swooping bats quickly thinned. He glanced back to see Jessica on the Ovaro's heels and steered the pinto closer to the rock wall to let her come alongside. "Go ahead of me," he shouted, drew back on the reins, and let her race ahead.

She turned into another passage in the rocks and Fargo followed, half turning in the saddle as he raised the big Henry. The Apache had seen their quarry turn into the passage and they were giving chase. Fargo had the rifle to his shoulder as two Apache ponies charged into view. He fired two shots, and both the Apache toppled from their ponies. Fargo turned and raced after Jessica, who had gone from sight as the passage took a sharp twist. As he rounded the turn he saw the figure sailing through the air from the top of the rocks, plummeting downward toward Jessica as she passed below. Bringing the rifle up in a sharp arc, Fargo fired two shots and saw the figure twist and shudder in midair as the bullets thudded into it.

The Apache was dead before his body, its trajectory shattered, landed against the side of the passage. Fargo raced the pinto after Jessica and caught up to her moments later as the passage broadened and led uphill again. "Slow down," he said as he reined in the Ovaro. There was no sound of pursuit from behind. They'd lost at least half of their band, and the Apache didn't take to night fighting. The horses brought to a trot and then a walk, Fargo moved on to where the passage ended and a half-dozen craters and rock depressions spread out before him. He circled two of the craters, found a small, shallow one, and pulled the pinto to a halt. "We'll bed down here," he said as he led the Ovaro down into the shallow depression of rock decorated by a half-dozen creosote bushes and one deformed acacia.

He took a blanket from his saddlebag and set it down. Shedding clothes, he shook his garments vigorously to rid them of the guano dust that had showered them. Out of the corner of his eye he saw Jessica enfold herself in a sheet before removing her clothes and spreading them out on the rocky floor. She lay down in the sheet across from him as he stretched out on the blanket, all but naked. He felt her eyes on him as he lay on his back and let his body relax.

"That was a terrible place," Jessica said softly.

"That's more often than not the way it is with hiding places," Fargo told her.

"And we almost didn't make it out," Jessica said. "But thanks anyway."

"For what?"

"For not making me stay, even though we might've been able to hide out," Jessica said, gratefulness in her voice.

"Sorry, honey, but you had nothing to do with it. The horses wouldn't stay quiet. That's why I decided to make a break for it," Fargo said.

She was silent for a moment. "I see," she said finally, her tone cool. "You're honest at least. I appreciate honesty."

He let a low chuckle escape him. "Do you, now?" he said.

"Good night, Fargo," she snapped and turned on her side, her back to him. He was still smiling when sleep rolled over him. The night stayed warm, the only sound that of the scorpions and eight-eyed wolf spiders scurrying along the hard rock floor of the crater on their quests for insects. He slept soundly, and the sun had come up when he pulled his eyes open, listened for a moment, heard nothing, and then sat up. The sheet where Jessica had lain was there, but she was gone. He frowned as he pulled on Levi's, stood up, and went to the Ovaro, where he drank sparingly from his canteen and let the horse drink some. He had just closed the canteen when he heard the scream—sudden, abrupt, more panic than pain in it.

The sound had come from beyond the low depression, and he ran up the side as it came again. Reaching the top, he swept the plateau of craters and depressed rock formations with a quick glance. The scream came once more, from just past a rib of layered rock. He ran forward, skirted the edge of the rock, and saw her at the bottom of a hole, up to her waist in water. She waved her arms and immediately sank deeper. "Hurry, I keep sinking," she cried out.

"Don't move," he said, spun, ran back to the Ovaro, and returned with his lariat. She had stayed quiet but had still sunk another few inches, he saw, and he flung the rope with his usual unerring accuracy. It landed over Jessica's head and shoulders and she grasped hold of it as he tightened the lariat around her. Unable to dig his heels into the rock, he sat down to give himself more balanced leverage as he pulled. She came free after a moment and helped him pull her up by half crawling, half scrambling up the side of the hole until she lay panting alongside him, breasts tightening against her tan shirt as she gulped in deep drafts of air. "How the hell'd you get here?" he growled.

"I woke up and decided to explore some," she said.

"All on your own. Not too smart," Fargo said.

"I didn't know I had to ask permission," she sniffed.

"Now you know," he grunted.

"I saw the water at the bottom and thought it was one of those *tinájas*," she explained.

"It wasn't. It was a sinkhole. There is underground water

below a sinkhole that undermines the surface. A little pressure makes them collapse. Sometimes they cave in all by themselves," Fargo said as he rose and pulled her to her feet.

"How do you tell the difference?" Jessica asked as she walked back beside him.

"By knowing what you're seeing," Fargo said. "There's a difference to the water and a difference to the rock. There's usually also a difference to the shape of the hole."

She paused at the gelding and the dark blue eyes studied him. "That's what makes a trailsman, isn't it? Knowing what you're seeing," she said.

"Bull's-eye," he said. "It comes in handy with women and horses, too."

"I hardly think they're similar," she said.

"You'd be surprised," he said, and she flashed a look of disagreement at him as he climbed onto the Ovaro. He rode south through the rock hills with Jessica at his side, ever watchful for signs of Apache. Finally the land led downward to a low plain. He came onto a growth of chufa before noon and showed Jessica how a tasty meal could be had with the nutty, sweet, juicy little tubers from the base of the plants. When they finished the meal, he led south again. The terrain grew less rocky, with a cover of mesquite, brittlebrush, and the soft sepia yellow of the paloverde trees. At the vestiges of a road, they came upon an old man with two burros loaded with hides.

"You must be wanting the Carronna place," he said in answer to Fargo's question. "There is a way station there and Carlos Carronna sells wagons. Stay on this road and you find it."

"Much obliged," Fargo said and put the pinto into a trot.

"You going to let me handle it this time?" Jessica asked as they rode.

"Why not?" he smiled. "Let's try the woman's touch."
She showed a moment of surprise at his willingness, and he
tossed her another affable smile. She had instantly assumed
his agreement to be a kind of concession, he realized, and
he was happy to let her think that. It was nothing of the
kind, of course. Fargo knew she'd not get anything from
the likes of a wily fox such as Carronna, but she could be
the diversion that might give him a chance to learn something. The buildings took shape by midafternoon, and as he
drew closer, Fargo saw a half-dozen sheds, a stable, a corral, and a fenced-in area alongside the sheds where a half-
dozen wagons rested. Across from the work buildings he
saw a stone-and-stucco building with a log roof and some
ten windows, the most substantial building of them all except for a small, solid cabin to one side. A wooden sign
hung over the doorway of the largest building and proclaimed in two languages: INN–FONDA

He paused and scanned the wagon yard with the adjacent
barn. He saw an Owensboro huckster wagon, a one-horse
farm wagon, a four-spring dray, and a closed-side light de-
livery wagon. None of the wagons were in very good
shape, and a number of pieces and parts, extra shafts, seat
beds, front gears, and slip tongues lay scattered about the
yard. Peering inside the shed, he saw a donkey cart. Fargo
rode to the front of the stone building and dismounted. A
half-dozen pigs came around one corner of the building
as a man stepped outside. He was of medium height, wearing a checked shirt, trousers, a neckerchief, and two pistols
that looked to be big five-shot, self-cocking Beaumont-
Adamses. Sharp, black, acquisitive eyes in a sallow, thin
face peered at Fargo from over a handlebar mustache. He
turned and fastened a glance on Jessica, instant appreciation in the sharp eyes.

"Buenas tardes," Fargo said, dismounting.

"Buenas tardes, amigo," the man said. "I am Carlos Carronna. What brings you to my little shop? You want a wagon, perhaps?"

"I'd say no, but we do want lodging, one night at least," Fargo said.

Carronna's eyes went to Jessica again, lingering on the corn-silk hair. "We have our best room for such a *hermosa* senorita," he said.

Jessica swung from the horse and tossed him a bright smile. "Very wonderful, a man who appreciates beauty," she said. "I'm Jessica Winter and this is Fargo." Fargo returned Carronna's offhanded nod and saw a woman come from the front door of the inn. She was perhaps thirty, Fargo guessed, thick black hair to her shoulders framing an attractive olive-skinned face with liquid black eyes and full lips that were all sensuality. A white scoop-necked blouse showed deep breasts that strained the fabric. She met his eyes and took in Jessica with one quick glance. She was followed outside by a youth, perhaps sixteen years old, carrying a big basket of laundry. Fargo instantly saw the pleasant but vacant stare of the retarded in the youth's eyes, the eye contact that wasn't really contact, and the somewhat uncoordinated movements of his body.

"Rosa, my housekeeper, and a very good cook," Carronna said. "And her brother, Pedro." The woman barely acknowledged Jessica and continued on with the boy, leading him to where a pump handle rose from a well some twenty yards away. "We have another well for drinking water just back of the house," Carronna said. "We have been fortunate in finding this spot, which lets us sell water to travelers who very badly need it."

"Lucky for everybody," Fargo said.

"Indeed. We ask only a modest sum for our services. Please, bring your things inside," Carronna said, and Jessica took her bag and followed him into the house. Fargo tagged along and saw Jessica shown to a room at the far end of a long corridor. As she entered the room, the man returned and took Fargo to a room at the other end of the corridor. "Will this be all right, Senor Fargo?" Carronna asked. He had mastered the veneer of the solicitous innkeeper, which didn't go at all with his greedy, acquisitive eyes, Fargo noted.

"This'll do fine. Any chance of getting a drink here?" Fargo asked.

"Mezcal . . . very fine mezcal," Carronna said.

"That'll do. See you in a few minutes," Fargo said and took his things into the room, where he found a washbasin beside the single chair and narrow bed. A small, high window admitted light into the room. He freshened up and changed his shirt. When he went outside, Rosa was at a long table in what was apparently the dining area. A bottle of mezcal and a glass were on the table.

"*Salud,* senor," the woman said.

"*Gracias,*" Fargo responded. "Can you sit and talk some?"

"No, I must see to Pedro. He will sit and dream if I don't stay on him," Rosa said.

"Maybe later, after dinner," Fargo said pleasantly, and she gave a half shrug that said nothing. Jessica came from the corridor as Fargo took a sip of the mezcal and sat down beside him, her voice low.

"If Carronna knows anything, I think I can get it out of him," she said.

"Do you, now?" Fargo said.

"Yes. You just go along with whatever I say," she instructed.

"Sure thing," he agreed.

"I'll have to be my most charming and bring him along.

I've seen his kind. A pretty woman can wrap him around her finger," Jessica said.

"Is that so?" Fargo said.

"Yes. And I won't make your mistake. I won't portray us as Indian-lovers while I find out what I want to know," Jessica said with loftiness.

Fargo shrugged and smiled and kept his thoughts to himself. Jessica wrapping Carronna around her finger was pretty much like a rabbit doing in a rattler. Yet something might come of it. He turned off the thought as Rosa entered, Pedro following with the basket of laundry. "What time is dinner?" Fargo queried.

"You can have dinner whenever you like. Carlos said so," Rosa replied as Pedro looked on with a dreamy half smile.

"Seven o'clock?" Jessica suggested.

"Fine," Rosa said and hurried on.

"I'm going to rest till then, unless you want me to help you with the horses," Jessica said to Fargo.

"I'll take care of the horses. An actress should rest before a performance," Fargo answered.

Jessica's eyes narrowed at him. "You don't think I can charm him into finding out what he knows, do you?" she said. "You don't think I can do it."

"I'm sure you can, and I'll be waiting for the results," Fargo said, finished the mezcal, and walked from the inn. He gathered the Ovaro and the tan gelding as Pedro came out a side door with a water bucket. "Hello," Fargo said gently as he decided to probe the boy a little. Pedro stopped and smiled in his dreamy way, a smile that was somehow very private.

"I am Pedro," he said. "Rosa is my sister."

"She's a very nice sister," Fargo said, and the youth nodded vigorously. He was definitely retarded, but he was functional, Fargo saw. "Where's the stable, Pedro?" Fargo asked, and Pedro pointed to the wagon shed.

"In there," Pedro said, and Fargo wondered whether the youth really made connections.

"You and Rosa have been here a long time?" Fargo asked, shifting tactics. Pedro nodded vigorously again. "How long?" Fargo queried.

The youth thought for a long moment. "Long time," he said.

"How long?" Fargo questioned again.

"Long time," Pedro repeated.

He was not good at defining time, Fargo decided. "I'll bet you watch everything that goes on around here, don't you, Pedro?" Fargo said.

Pedro's smile widened. "Yes, I watch everything," he said and started for the nearest well. Fargo walked with him until he halted at the well, and then led the horses to the wagon shed, uncertain what he'd find. But at the rear of the shed he found a six-stall stable and put the horses next to each other. He had time to give both horses a quick rubdown with a dandy brush, and when he finished, night had crept over the land. He walked to the inn after washing at the well pump and found the main table set with clay dishes and Jessica sitting across from Carronna, who poured wine from a jug.

Four men sat at a separate table, two plainly Mexican, two not, all hard-faced and hard-eyed and wearing rough work outfits and six-guns. Pedro sat by himself at another table set for two, Fargo noted. "Senor Fargo, we have been waiting for you," Carronna said.

"Some more guests?" Fargo asked with a nod to the four men.

"No, no," Carronna said with a laugh. "These hombres

work for me. It may not seem it, but there is a lot to do in a place like this. And then I need guards."

"Guards?" Fargo queried.

"Yes. There are plenty of bandidos who come this way. I need guards, amigo," Carronna said.

Jessica cut in. "Well, I'm here to enjoy Senor Carronna, not talk about bandidos," she said. "And to see if the senor can help me." She flashed a bright smile and Carronna beamed.

"Carlos, please call me Carlos," he said.

"If you'll call me Jessica," she said as Rosa appeared with a tray holding a platter of hot sliced meat atop a bed of rice. She served Jessica first, then Carronna, and then stopped at Fargo's plate before returning to the kitchen. Fargo took a long sip of the wine and found it better than he'd expected. He took a bite of the sliced meat and rice, let the taste cling to his mouth, and savored the sweetish flavor.

"Iguana," he said, and Carronna applauded.

"The senor knows his game," he said and refilled everyone's glass. Fargo sat back, enjoying the meal as Jessica continued to concentrate charm and vivaciousness on Carronna, who clearly enjoyed the attention. The wine seemed to be loosening his tongue as his laughter grew louder and his compliments came faster. Jessica's performance would have turned the heads of most of the men she knew, Fargo conceded silently. But he also saw that Carronna's eyes stayed sharp, no wine-soaked relaxation in their darting inquisitiveness.

Fargo saw the four hands finish their meal and leave the room while Rosa still sat with Pedro, who ate slowly, with deliberate movements. It was soon after that Carronna gave Jessica the opening she wanted. "What brings such a lovely senorita to this devil's land?" he asked.

Jessica let her face grow troubled. "Searching," she said.

"For my cousin. She looks a little like me, and I am very afraid for her." Carronna frowned in sympathy at once, and Jessica leaned closer to him. "She came out here with a friend, and word came to me that she may have been taken prisoner. Even worse, she may have fallen into the hands of a slave trader, a man called Lucas DeLora. I came to try and find her and hired Fargo, here, to help me. Now I'm hoping you can help. Perhaps this slave trader has passed this way."

Carronna frowned in thought. "I don't know. A lot of people pass this way. You'd be surprised," he said. Fargo's eyes were not on Carronna but on the nearby table as Pedro turned in his chair, his eyes widening. He started to raise one arm, but Rosa's hand shot out, yanking the youth's head by the hair. Still holding onto him, she hissed something into the boy's ear, and Pedro returned his attention to his plate. "I'd have to think back on everyone who's come by," Carronna's voice drifted to Fargo. "Maybe you could tell me more about your cousin, help me remember her or something more."

"Of course," Jessica said.

"But let us talk over some more wine. I'll get another jug," Carronna said and hurried into the kitchen. Fargo leaned over to Jessica.

"I don't see you needing me here," he said.

"You're right. It might be better if I were alone with him. He might talk more freely with just me there," Jessica agreed.

"Exactly what I was thinking," Fargo said and pushed away from the table. He cast a glance at Rosa. She was clearing away dishes, Pedro helping, and Fargo wandered from the inn as Carronna returned with the second jug of wine. Outside, he moved quickly, with short, stealthy steps, to a window that let him peer into the kitchen. Rosa was talking to the youth, her face stern, and she held his face in both hands to make certain he listened to her. Finally she stopped, dropped her hands from his face, and began to do the dishes as Pedro took a towel to dry them.

Fargo slid himself along the outside wall of the house until he found another window that was open in the warm night. He lifted first one then the other long leg over the sill and swung inside the house, where he paused in the darkened interior. He could see down the corridor into the clay kitchen, where he watched Rosa lead the boy to a room off a side corridor. She went into the room with Pedro, closing the door behind, and Fargo waited a few moments before he moved closer. He could hear the faint voices of Jessica and Carronna from the front section of the building as he moved on cat's feet down the side corridor.

Pausing before Rosa's room, he thought about knocking but decided against it. He turned the doorknob slowly and the door opened. Rosa turned as he stepped into the room, surprise sweeping her face. Clad only in a thin white nightdress, her deep breasts with their large, dark circles pressed into the material. "Please, don't be afraid," Fargo said. A lamp on low showed him a large room with a bed, dresser, quilt rug, and three chairs. A drape covered an arched entrance to an adjoining room.

"What do you want?" Rosa asked warily.

"Just to talk," he said and nodded toward the draped doorway. "Pedro in there?" he asked.

"Yes. That is his room," Rosa said as her eyes searched his face. "What do you want to talk about?"

"When Jessica asked about the slave trader, DeLora, Pedro turned to say something. You stopped him. Why?" Fargo questioned.

Caution came into the woman's big, liquid eyes. "Carlos does not like Pedro to talk to guests," she said.

"Try again," Fargo said.

Rosa looked away. "There was nothing else," she said.

"Maybe I should ask Pedro," Fargo suggested, and Rosa spun on him with instant protectiveness.

"You stay away from Pedro," she snapped.

"Then talk to me, Rosa. Maybe you can help me. Maybe we can help each other. What was Pedro going to say when you stopped him?" Fargo pressed.

Rosa stared back, thoughts racing behind the liquid eyes as she studied him. "Will you take Pedro and me away from here?" she asked.

"Hadn't thought about it." Fargo said and let his eyes study her. "Are you Carlos's woman?" he asked.

"That *cochino*?" Rosa hissed.

"He doesn't seem like a man who'd take no for an answer, especially when he's in charge," Fargo remarked.

"You are right. One of these days he will break our agreement. I know that *zoquete*," Rosa spit out.

"Agreement?" Fargo echoed.

"When my mother died, it was left to me to look after Pedro. You have seen he is not like most people. Others would have put him away someplace, but I could not do that. But it is hard to take care of someone like Pedro. Most people do not want him around."

"I'm sure it's hard," Fargo said.

"I was desperate to take care of Pedro. Carlos Carronna was desperate to find a housekeeper and cook. I agreed to work for him if he let me keep Pedro with me. That was our agreement. But I did not know he would bring me to this hellhole of a place."

"You ask anyone else to help you get away?" Fargo questioned.

"I would not ask most of those who come this way. It would be like jumping from the frying pan into the fire. But you and the senorita are different." She stepped closer, her hand reaching out to rest on his arm. "I have to get away with Pedro. I know as soon as Carlos gets someone else, some *muchacha*, I am finished. But he will take me, first, and kill Pedro."

"Has he killed anyone here?" Fargo asked.

"I did not see it, but there have been travelers who have never left. They just seemed to disappear, two of them women," Rosa said. "I must get away from here. I've saved enough, from tips mostly, to live until I can find a new place for myself and Pedro—maybe in Socorro."

Fargo frowned at Rosa. "Those are all good reasons for you to get away from here. Give me a good reason to help you."

"You drive a hard bargain, Fargo," Rosa said.

"It's a hard world. Tell me what Pedro was going to say when you stopped him," Fargo said.

Rosa's lips tightened for a moment but she gave a resigned shrug, the deep breasts lifting to press the large, dark circles tight against the nightgown for an instant. "He was going to contradict Carlos. That's why I stopped him. He was going to say that the slave trader had been here," Rosa said.

"Lucas DeLora?"

"Yes. He has stopped this way often. This time he had three men and two wagons with him," Rosa said.

Fargo leaned forward as excitement pulled at him. "Did you see the women he had with him?" he asked.

"No, he kept the women in his wagons—two farm wagons with special canvas tops."

"Women?" Fargo frowned. "How do you know there was more than one?"

"They had me cook enough food for three, at least," Rosa said.

"But you never saw any of them?" Fargo pressed.

"Never."

"Did Pedro?"

"No, the men kept everyone away from the wagons," Rosa said.

"Do you know which way they went when they left?" Fargo questioned and saw Rosa's face grow set.

"No more—not till you tell me you'll take us out of here," she said.

Fargo hesitated for a moment. "That won't be easy. I'll have to find a way."

"Whatever you say we'll do. You are my hope to get away," Rosa said.

"First I want to talk to Jessica. It may take me until the morning to think of a way," Fargo told her.

"We can wait. We are used to waiting," Rosa said, and he nodded at her as he slipped from the room and hurried down the side corridor. There were no voices from the front of the inn, and he paused to see only the wine jug and half-filled glasses on the table. A large candle was burning low and the room was dim as he crossed the floor to the main corridor. He strode to Jessica's room, opened the door, and saw only the empty room. He hissed a curse and spun on his heel, listened as he half ran down the corridor but heard nothing from any of the rooms.

He swore again as he knew exactly what had happened. Carronna had persuaded her to go somewhere with him and she'd agreed, still naively certain she was running the show. "Damn-fool girl," Fargo muttered as he burst into Rosa's room. She sat up in the bed, deep breasts bouncing. "Jessica's gone with him. Where'd he take her?" Fargo bit out.

"There's a little hut, adobe, behind the main shed," Rosa said.

"Get your stuff together," Fargo flung back as he raced out of the room. He heard Rosa swinging from the bed as he streaked down the corridor.

5

He raced outside, past the large shed and stable, and noted a barrackslike structure behind the inn. Slowing, he spotted the adobe hut and saw the sliver of lamplight from beneath the door. He halted, pressed himself to the door, and it was Jessica's voice he heard first. "I never did. I never promised you anything," she said.

"You think you can wave yourself at Carlos Carronna and he falls into your lap, bitch?" Carronna's voice answered, followed by a harsh laugh.

"You let me go and I won't say anything about this," Jessica said.

"And not enjoy myself? That would be criminal, and such a waste. I don't like little *putas* who think they are smarter than Carlos Carronna."

"You can't get away with this, you slimy pig," Jessica said, and Fargo heard the sound of a slap and her sharp cry.

"Bitch," Carronna snarled. Fargo left the door and stepped to a small window, where he had to stretch onto his toes to see into the hut. Carronna was dragging Jessica from a chair to a cot, a rope around her that bound her arms to her sides. Her shirt hung open to reveal the side of one curving, creamy white breast. Carronna threw her down on the cot and put one knee into her stomach. "Look what I've got for you, fancy senorita," he said, fumbling at his trousers.

"No, oh, God, please, no," Jessica gasped, and now there was only terror in her voice. Fargo drew back from the window, yanked his Colt from its holster, and turned the gun so he gripped it by the barrel. He didn't want shots that would being the others running. He'd have only one chance to reach Carronna and it had to be quick and noiseless. He reached the door as he heard Jessica scream, turned the doorknob as he put his shoulder to the door, and catapulted himself into the hut.

Carronna was half atop her, pushing her legs apart with one of his, his trousers around his ankles. He turned as he heard the sound at the door and tried to reach the holster that lay with his trousers. Fargo was across the room with one long stride. He brought the butt of the Colt down across Carronna's forehead and a streak of blood appeared as the man collapsed onto his pants. Fargo stepped over Carronna, yanked Jessica to her feet, and undid the rope around her.

"Oh, God, thank you, thank you," she said, clinging to him, yet instantly pulling her shirt closed. "How did you know he had me here?"

"Rosa told me," Fargo said and pushed her out the doorway. Carronna would come around all too quickly, he knew. Fargo halted as he saw Rosa and Pedro waiting beside two quarter horses, cloth bags slung across each of them. "They're coming with us," he said at Jessica's frown. "Get your things and then get the horses."

"What are you going to do?" she asked.

"See that Carronna and his men don't come chasing after us," Fargo said, and Jessica hurried to the stable shed. "Where are the other horses?" he asked Rosa.

"In the corral," she said.

"Let them out, open the gate," he said, and she gave orders to Pedro in Spanish. As the boy hurried to the corral in his uncoordinated gait, Fargo took Rosa with him into the inn. "Candles, torches, kerosene lamps," he said, and Rosa hurried off to return with three candles and two kerosene lamps. She disappeared and came back with two long poles, soaked at the ends with oil. "Light them," he said as they left the house and hurried outside. Pedro was beside the corral gate, trying to shoo the horses out, when Fargo took one of the torches and plunged it into a pile of dry wood chips and straw alongside the corral fence.

The fire leaped upward at once. He handed the torches to Rosa, who began to set fire to another corner of the corral fence. The horses suddenly began to panic, rearing up first, screams of fear coming from three of them. Then they bolted from the corral, rushing through the gate. Fargo flung one of the kerosene lamps against the door of the inn, where it instantly exploded into flame. He saw Jessica coming from the shed with the Ovaro and the gelding, ran past her, and smashed the second lamp into the shed. The dry wood caught at once, a spiral of flame leaping upward. It would take but minutes for the entire shed and wagons to be consumed.

But he heard another sound as he lighted one of the candles and set it against a small shed—voices shouting, and then, from the adobe hut, the sound of a shot. He saw Carronna's figure come stumbling out of the hut, firing wildly, and from the barracks, the four men rushing out. "Hit the saddle," he said and saw Jessica swing onto the gelding as Rosa and Pedro took to their horses. Jessica sent the Ovaro at him and he caught the horse's reins and pulled himself into the saddle. "Stay low," he called out as he sent the Ovaro into a gallop as a hail of shots split the night. The horses from the corral were already racing away into the night, and he heard Carronna's voice screaming over the shots. "Never mind them. Water, buckets, get water," the man shouted. But some of the men continued to shoot, and Fargo had just passed Pedro when he heard the boy's cry.

"Rosa . . . ow, ow, Rosa . . . I am hit, I am hit," Pedro gasped out. Fargo reined to a halt, swung the Ovaro around as Rosa circled back to come alongside Pedro as the youth slumped forward in the saddle. "It hurts, Rosa . . . oh, it hurts," Pedro cried.

"Ride with him. I'll take your horse," Fargo said as he saw two of Carronna's men running toward him to take a closer shot. But they were perfectly outlined by the fires burning behind them, and Fargo took aim at the nearest one. He fired and the figure did a little skipping step before it collapsed. The second man dived to the ground and rolled as Fargo's next shot caught him in the calf. He let out a scream of pain as he tried to roll into a ball. But Fargo had already swung the Ovaro around as he scooped up the reins of Rosa's horse and led the way into the darkness. He glanced back to see Carronna and two of his men tossing buckets of water from the wells at buildings that were already too wreathed in flames to save. It'd take them a day, at least, to round up the horses, he guessed, perhaps more. He came alongside Jessica and Rosa, who cradled Pedro as she rode.

Pedro was whimpering against Rosa but he was sitting the horse well enough. "We'll stop soon," Fargo said and followed the dry, flat land under a half-moon until he spied an arroyo and led the way inside it. He halted, swung from the pinto, and helped lift the youth from the horse. "Let's have a look at it," he said as he saw the stain of red on Pedro's shirt. He examined the wound after opening Pedro's shirt. Rosa looked on. "The bullet cracked one of his upper ribs. But it passed through. He'll have sore ribs for a while but he'll be all right," Fargo said. "I'd say he can ride if we take it easy."

"I've some cloth to make a bandage in my bag," Rosa said.

"Get it," Fargo said, and let Rosa do the rest as she bandaged the youth with thin strips of cotton. He walked to where Jessica waited beside a tall slab of stone.

"I'm sorry about Carronna. I'd no idea he was going to act like that," she said.

"It seems you ran out of charm. Didn't exactly wrap him around your little finger, did you?" Fargo remarked and drew a half glare. "Why'd you go to the hut with him?"

"He said he kept his records there, names and times of people who stopped there," she said.

"And you swallowed it hook, line, and sinker," Fargo grunted.

"I didn't know he was going to turn into a monster," she protested.

"He didn't turn into anything he wasn't already," Fargo said.

"It doesn't really make any difference. He doesn't know anything. I'm convinced of that," Jessica said with a return of loftiness.

"Why?" Fargo asked blandly.

"I questioned him pretty closely before we went to his hut. I didn't catch any sign that he was lying or holding back," she said.

"You didn't catch any sign he was going to screw you in his hut, either," Fargo said.

"I was wrong about that, damn it," she snapped.

"You were wrong about everything. DeLora stopped there, more than once," Fargo said.

Jessica's mouth fell open. "How do you know that?"

"Rosa told me," he said. "You see, a good liar can always fool you. That's why you often learn more by watching the people around him who aren't as clever or as good liars. That's why I let you play your little charade with Carronna. I knew you weren't going to charm a damn thing out of him. I wanted to watch those around him."

She was silent for a long moment, and he saw her lips were tight as she answered. "You could've told me that's how you felt," she said, resentment in her eyes.

"Why? You'd have only argued about it, then," he said, and she turned away as Rosa approached with Pedro.

"We're ready," Rosa said and saw that Pedro was back atop his horse. Fargo nodded, took to the saddle, and led the way out of the arroyo. He rode till almost morning, when he came upon a line of volcanic hollows that made a good spot to bed down, one a *caldera* holding rainwater.

"We'll talk in the morning," he told Rosa, and she agreed with a nod. Jessica found a small hollow for herself, and Fargo settled down in a larger crater where Rosa and Pedro took one side. He slept at once and stayed asleep until after the sun rose. He woke when the rocks began to burn with heat and saw Rosa just sitting up, drawing on a blouse that tightened around the deep, full breasts. "You brought water, I hope," he called to her.

"Yes, four canteens," she said and watched him as he rose and let the sun bathe his smoothly muscled body for a few moments. Jessica appeared when he'd finished dressing and halted beside Pedro.

"How are your ribs?" she asked.

"They hurt, senorita," the youth said, but managed a smile.

"You've things to tell me, Rosa," Fargo said as he walked the horses to the *caldera* and let them drink.

"Yes, Fargo, and many thanks to give you," Rosa said.

"Some would have left Pedro behind when the shooting came."

"Tell me about DeLora," he said. "You must've overheard talk between him and Carronna if he made regular stops there."

"Yes, he has a place where he keeps the women, near the Gila River at the foot of the Superstition Mountains, a place called Hard Springs."

"That'd be in Arizona territory," Fargo said.

"The last time he said he had a special customer coming," Rosa said.

"Good enough," Fargo nodded. "Now we ride hard," he said and made good on his words as he set a pace as fast as the heat and the strength of the horses would allow. They made good time and by nightfall had crossed the Pecos. Fargo found a spot to camp on the other side of the river where a stand of smooth sumac interrupted the paloverde. It had been a particularly hard ride for Pedro, and he ate lightly and immediately fell asleep after Rosa changed his bandage. "We'll reach Socorro tomorrow," Fargo told her.

"That is good. I thank you, Fargo," Rosa said, her liquid eyes searching his face. "You are a good man, and a handsome one. I am sorry I will have such a short time with you. The senorita is *afortunado*."

"*Gracias*," he laughed. "But the senorita is *mucho puro*, too *puro* to be *afortunado*."

"That will be her loss." Rosa smiled. "*Buenas nochas*, Fargo." He watched her go into the sumac near where Pedro had found a spot, then took the Ovaro, passed Jessica where she lay under a light sheet near the shoreline, and went on further. He halted at the edge of the sumac and shed clothes and lay down on his bedroll. The half-moon moved slowly across the sky. He watched the deep blue curtain behind it and was almost asleep when he heard the footsteps. His hand closed around the big Colt at his side and he squinted into the night to see the figure move toward him from the edge of the river. The moonlight caught at the folds of the nightgown, and he sat up as Rosa halted beside him, her eyes traveling up and down his nakedness. *"Magnifico,"* she breathed and sank down on her knees beside him. "I surprise you, Fargo?"

"A little. But it is a nice surprise," Fargo said.

"You were good to save Pedro, and take us away—and it is a long time since I have seen a man like you. I do not know what the world will bring after Socorro. I deserve some pleasure now. And you do, too, my friend," Rosa said.

"Maybe so," Fargo agreed, and Rosa lifted the nightgown and let it drop beside her. He let his eyes linger on the full, deep breasts, bordering on pendulousness but managing to avoid it. Large dark red nipples protruded from equally dark red areolas, and below her breasts, a fleshy layer padded a deep rib cage and a convex belly. Rosa's thighs held more flesh than they needed, yet they were not without shape, tapering to round knees and strong but attractive calves. His eyes held on a black triangle of totally sensuous bushiness, thick and deep, made for plunging one's hand into to caress the soft, wiry curls and press the very round pubic mound.

He felt his body reacting at once to the complete sensuality of her, an earthy, raw eroticism of simmering flesh. She was upon him as he rose, pressing the deep breasts into his face, pillows of delightful smothering. One dark red nipple found his lips, and he pulled at it gently. Rosa made low, rumbling noises from deep down inside herself. "Good . . . oh, good . . . *maravilloso* . . . oh, *sí, sí,* yes, yes," she breathed, moving from one language to another. He felt the soft, round belly come against his hardness, press down on him, and he turned with her, his mouth staying on one deep breast, his hand exploring down across the black, deep bushiness, pressing hard on the triangle, feeling the soft pubic mound underneath seem to press back against him.

Rosa was uttering words, disconnected words, but the passion in them was the same. His hand moved down from the dense triangle and he felt the wetness of her inner thighs, welcoming passage made more welcome. He moved his hand to the soft lips, the lubricious portal, and Rosa growled, a deep, throbbing sound that gave voice to the sensations of the flesh. He touched, probed, went deeper, and her thighs hung open for him, slapped together against him, and fell open again as her ample hips rose upward, sought, demanded, and fell back to thrust upward again. *"Por favor, por favor,"* Rosa gasped, and her hands were pulling him to her, clasping around his back. He shifted, rose, came forward, slid into her, and Rosa's growling sounds grew louder.

"Sí, sí, oh, so good, so good," she muttered, and her hips moved for him, with him, finding a wonderful rhythm that grew wilder, harder, until it was a thing of its own. He felt himself swept along with the no-nonsense, earthy abandon that was Rosa, her total, raw enjoyment allowing for no subtleties, no patient lovemaking. But her complete immersion in pleasure made up for everything else. He felt the round belly begin to slap against his groin with quick motions. *"Ahora, ahora, ahora,"* she half screamed.

"Now, now," he echoed and felt his own climax erupting with hers, and then he was wrapped around her in the final thrusting spasms of utter desire. The world flashed, vanished, exploded back into reality, and finally Rosa sank back and he was clinging to her, hearing her long, shuddering gasps. "Too good, Fargo, too good," Rosa breathed.

"Never too good," he said.

Her smile was slow. "You are right—never too good," she said. "But I will remember this and remember you, *amigo*. I will remember Fargo." She turned to lie close against him and slept quickly, and he closed his eyes to stay with her until she woke when dawn began to creep across the sky. She left silently, carrying the nightgown, her earthy figure disappearing down the shoreline. He returned to sleep and woke with the sun full on the land. He washed and dressed and went to where the others were preparing to ride. Jessica fastened him with a disdainful glance as he passed that made him lift an eyebrow. But he said nothing and led the way from the sumac and back across the hard, dry land where the saguaro cactus stood as strange, giant sentinels.

They reached the town of Socorro soon after midday. It was a dry, dusty town, but there were stores and some houses and there was an air of solidarity. "This will do," Rosa said approvingly. "We will find a place here, and if not, we will go on. I saw a stage depot."

"Good luck, Rosa, for you and Pedro," Fargo said.

"Thank you, Fargo," she said and turned to Jessica. "Good luck, senorita."

"Good luck to you," Jessica said, and if she tried to keep the stiffness out of her voice, she failed, Fargo noted.

"Ride," he barked at her and set the Ovaro into a fast trot. He stayed in a trot as they left Socorro and rode west across the hot terrain. He stayed west, except to dip down to avoid the big forest the Apache claimed as their own. A trickle of a stream appeared and he halted to water the horses and watch Jessica as she refilled her canteen. When she finished, his voice was hard. "You haven't said a word to me since we left the Pecos, and it damn near broke your little ass to be polite to Rosa. Give it some words, honey," he said.

Her dark blue eyes were cool under the thin, arched eyebrows as they turned to him. "I've nothing to say," she answered.

"Steer shit, honey," he growled.

"Let's say I don't approve of expecting payment for doing a good," she said icily.

"You want to add to that?" Fargo frowned.

"I couldn't sleep last night. I went for a stroll along the river. I couldn't help hearing," Jessica said.

Fargo let a small whistle escape his lips. "You're making a career out of being wrong," he said.

"I wasn't wrong. I couldn't mistake what I heard," she snapped.

"Not wrong about that. Wrong about expecting payment. I wasn't expecting. It just happened—Rosa's idea more than mine."

"But you were perfectly willing to accept," she said. "Did you expect that kind of gratitude from me? After all, you did save my life at the sinkhole and with Carronna."

"No. Never considered it," he said.

"Never?"

"Never."

He saw the little furrow slide across her brow as she peered at him. "Why not?" she asked.

He smiled. "You're sounding disappointed."

She instantly drew indignation around herself. "I'm nothing of the kind. I'm simply curious," she said.

"Guess you'll have to stay curious. Can't give you an answer," he said.

"Can't or won't?"

"Your pick," he shrugged.

"Perhaps you're only attracted to certain types of women," she said loftily.

"Maybe," he shrugged again.

"I wouldn't expect you to be so selective," she sniffed.

"Guess you're wrong again. You're setting a record," he returned blandly, turned away, and pulled himself onto the Ovaro. "Let's ride," he said. She swung in beside him, but the anger was out of her face, he noted, and he smiled inwardly. The day ended soon after, and he halted beside a rock formation of tall pillars. They ate from their beef strips, and Jessica undressed behind one of the rocks, returning in a light sheet she'd wrapped around herself. He'd shed clothes and lay nearly naked on his bedroll. She settled down near him, and he saw her eyes move across his body.

"You think DeLora still has Moonrise?" Jessica asked.

"That's anybody's guess," Fargo said.

"If he does, how do we get her away from him? It sounds as though he's running a fair-sized operation. He won't be alone," Jessica said.

"That's right," Fargo agreed.

"You think you can sneak in or fight your way in and take her?" Jessica pressed.

"That'd be the high-risk way, a last resort," Fargo said.

"So what are you thinking?" she frowned.

"I'm thinking I'll make you a madam," he said blandly, and saw Jessica sit up, her lips parting. She caught the sheet just before it fell from her breasts.

6

"What are you saying? That's ridiculous. I don't look like a madam," Jessica protested.

"You ever see a madam?" he asked.

"Well, no," she said.

"They come in all sizes, shapes, and colors," Fargo said.

"But they wear tight dresses and cheap makeup, don't they?"

"Only at work. It's plain that DeLora sells the girls he takes. That's what makes him a slave trader. I'd guess his special girls, such as Moonrise, are only a small part of his trade. I'm going to go in as a high roller looking to open a brothel, and you're going to be my madam. I brought you along so you could pick and choose," Fargo explained.

"How disgusting. The very idea nauseates me. It's sickening," Jessica said.

"But you're going to do it. Forty men, women, and children's lives depend on our finding Moonrise," Fargo said. She lay back and he heard the deep sigh of discontent come from her. "Go to sleep. The days will only get harder," he said, turned on his side, and pulled slumber to him.

When the new day dawned, he woke first and glanced across at her. The sheet had come loose to show the beautiful long curve of one lovely leg, skin of unblemished smoothness, and a knee perfectly rounded. He rose and used his canteen to wash. She woke as he finished dressing. She sat up, shook the corn-silk hair, and looked improperly lovely. She dressed behind a rock as he saw to the horses, and her face was still set as she emerged, dressed, from behind the rock.

"I don't like it any better after sleeping on it," she said. "I don't think I can pull it off. I can't fool a man such as DeLora." Fargo's jaw tightened at the truth in her words.

"You're going to have to fool him. It's our only way in," he said.

"What if I'm right? What if he sees through me?" Jessica said.

"We play it by ear, then," Fargo said tersely and swung onto the pinto. He set a strong pace that left no time for more talking, kept it up through the day, and camped at the bottom of a small cut when the night came. Jessica found a paloverde to undress behind and once again lay down nearby in the sheet. He lay on his back in the hot night, letting his near nakedness cool his body, aware that her eyes lingered on him. Tiredness pulled at him, and he closed his eyes as sleep began to take hold. He was almost drifting off when he heard her voice, a soft, hissed gasp.

"Oh . . . oh, my God . . . oh . . ."

He snapped his eyes open and looked over at her. She lay on her back, one arm out of the sheet, and it took him a moment before he saw the movement atop the sheet. "Shit," he murmured as the movement took shape. It seemed to be a coil of rope, only he knew better. The shape moved again, an "S" movement across the sheet, and Fargo saw the slightly horned head of the Sonora sidewinder. His hand crept toward the Colt in the holster lying at his side. "Don't move. Don't even breathe," he whispered and saw Jessica's eyes staring upward. Luckily for her, she was too terrified to move. But that wouldn't last, he knew. He slowly drew the gun from the holster. "Don't move," he whispered again.

The rattlesnake slid forward again with its distinctive winding motion, its forked tongue flicking out, seeking the warmth of the living prey with its heat sensors. The Sonora sidewinder hunted at night. Its venom was fast working, destroying the coagulants in the victim's blood and causing fatal hemorrhaging. It would be only seconds longer before the rattler's sensors zeroed in on Jessica's exposed arm. Fargo half-turned on his side, lifted the Colt, and aimed. He'd have but one shot, fired over Jessica, too close to her chest. If he missed, the snake would strike, an automatic reaction. He couldn't miss, he told himself, and let the rattler's head come into the gun sight. He pressed the trigger, ever so slightly, making certain the gun didn't pull.

The shot split the air and he saw the rattler's head blow apart. The snake's body leaped upward reflexively and Jessica screamed, rolled, took the sheet with her, and came up against him. "Oh, God, oh, my God," she breathed, her arms around his neck.

"It's over. You're all right, safe," he said as she continued to cling to him, the fright still in her face. But the sheet stayed around her, except for her arms, and it was Fargo who stepped back. He patted one round, bare, smooth shoulder with an almost avuncular touch. "You can go back to sleep now. You'll be fine," he said.

Her eyes stayed on him. "Thanks to you," she said. "Again."

"That's what friends are for," he smiled and walked away from her, picked up the body of the snake, and flung it behind the rocks. When she settled down her eyes were still on him, and he saw the little furrow on her brow. "Something bothering you?" he asked mildly.

"No. I guess I should thank you for not taking advantage of my gratitude," she said.

"Don't give it a second thought," Fargo said.

"Well, we've talked about your attraction to certain types of women. You're consistent, and there's something to be said for consistency."

"But you're still curious," he slid at her.

"Yes, or perhaps more surprised," Jessica said.

"Good, 'cause you're sounding disappointed again," he remarked.

"I assure you I'm not," she said, bristling at once.

"Good. Now get back to sleep. You'll need all of it you can get," he said.

"Yes, of course," she said as she lay down in the sheet with her back to him. There was a grimness to the smile he held inside himself. She was becoming more annoyed, frustrated, wrestling with emotions new to her and behavior trained into her from childhood. And in true female fashion, she was rebelling at being turned down, displaying more vanity than wanting. But it was putting a hell of a strain on his own self-discipline, though he wasn't about to tell her as much. He pulled sleep around himself again, and this time he didn't wake till the morning sun came.

He set another hard day's pace, and they reached the base of Superstition Mountain at midafternoon, the towering formation one of stone and more stone, tall spire of lava cooled millions of years ago and craters equally ancient. It was a harsh, bleak, unattractive place marked by the spots where man had attempted to find gold hidden in the vast towers of stone. It was a place where only the mountain rams felt at home. Fargo wound his way along the base, where bristlebrush and paloverde trees mingled with rows of purple-red flowers of the hedgehog cacti in bloom. The small collection of adobe and stone buildings came into view. He knew he had found Hard Springs and Lucas De-Lora's spread the minute he saw the fences of bristling barbed wire. As they approached the tall gate, three men came from inside, two carrying rifles, one wearing a six-gun.

"We don't take visitors, folks," the one with the six-gun said. He was a tall, thin man with hollowed cheeks and a general air of seediness. "We'd appreciate you moving on."

"We've come to see Lucas DeLora," Fargo said.

The man's brows lifted a fraction. "You got names?" he questioned.

"Fargo . . . Skye Fargo, and Miss Winter," the Trailsman said.

"Mister DeLora doesn't see people who just ride up. Send him a letter," the man said.

"I aim to do business with him. Carlos Carronna sent me," Fargo said, and the man's brows lifted a little further.

"Wait here," he said and strode away toward the largest of the buildings, a square, flat-roofed structure. Fargo let his eyes move across the building to the far right, where the almost solid wall was broken up by three small, high, barred windows. The two men with the rifles stayed in place, guns ready, both hard-eyed figures. One, wearing a flat-topped hat over long black hair, kept flicking glances at Jessica. Finally the tall, thin figure reappeared and barked orders at the other two, who quickly opened the gate. "Mister DeLora says you can come in," the man said and led the way to what was obviously the main house.

As they followed in the lowering light, Fargo took note of a stable and a work shed, along with another smaller square structure with small barred windows. The guard brought them inside the house. They stepped into a wide entranceway and saw a large, beefy man waiting there. He had thick lips in a fat face with heavy jowls, beetle brows, and large ears, brown hair slicked down over them. Only his eyes were small, almost tiny in the large face. Lucas DeLora wore a checked vest over a white shirt and sported a gold watch chain across his chest. Fargo saw the man's eyes bore into him, then Jessica, curiosity and shrewd caution in their dark depths.

"Fargo and Miss Winter, is it? I am surprised," DeLora said.

"At what?" Fargo asked. "That we found you?"

"That Carronna should send you. He knows I do not see people," the man said.

"We convinced him you'd be happy to see us," Fargo said. "We've real money to spend."

DeLora gave them both another long, thoughtful glance and then motioned to them. "Since you are here, come inside," he said and showed them into a large living room with a thick rug on the floor and heavy drapes on the windows. Solid furniture filled the room, one piece a sofa of heavy, gold-flecked material on which DeLora folded his considerable bulk. "What made you come visit me with money?" the man asked with an offhand air.

Fargo allowed a smile as Jessica sat down on the edge of a heavy chair. "Come on, now, friend. You don't work in secret. We've been asking around, talking to people. We kept getting your name. You see, we're going to open up a place. I'll bankroll it, Miss Winter will run it. But no ordinary place. We want only special girls for big-money customers. We heard you were the man to see for that."

"Where do you figure to open up?" Lucas DeLora asked.

"Oh, I'm thinking Texas, near Houston," Fargo said expansively. "I'll spend top dollar, but only for special girls. I want to develop a fancy clientele. I heard you had yourself a Kiowa virgin, daughter of a chief. Now that's the kind of girl I want."

"Where'd you hear about her?" DeLora asked, suspicion quick to touch his voice.

"You think you operate in secret, my friend?" Fargo laughed. DeLora didn't join in. "Somebody always talks. I came especially about her," Fargo went on.

"You're too late by a couple of days. She's gone," DeLora said. "One of my special buyers picked her up."

Fargo let himself frown in disappointment. "I'm real sorry to hear that. I'd be willing to buy her from whoever's got her," he offered.

"No chance, Mister Fargo. The man's an old and valuable customer of mine, everything ordered custom-picked, and he comes a goddamn long way to get something special. Forget about the little squaw," DeLora said. "I've got some other very special girls you can have at the right price, and eight ordinary ones to get you started in business."

"Guess we'll have to do without the Indian girl," Fargo said. "But I'm real disappointed. I don't think you've anything else that special. Tell me the truth, now."

"I've got two real special girls, both not over fifteen, both untouched. Now, that's hard to come by," DeLora said.

"That's true enough, though I'm thinking I'd like to sleep on it," Fargo said. Then Jessica's voice cut in.

"We're not buying any girls I haven't seen," she said icily. "I want to see what you've got, first." Fargo just managed to keep the surprise from flooding his face. He shot a quick glance at Jessica. All he saw was the ice in her face, barely containing her fury. DeLora was studying her with hardness in his tiny eyes.

"Got to give in to my partner," Fargo said quickly, keeping an expansive affability in his voice. "I want her to be satisfied."

DeLora grunted as he pulled his girth up and started toward the door. Jessica followed close behind him, and Fargo hurried after her as the man led the way from the house. He crossed through the dusk toward the square structure with the small barred windows. Fargo took note of the two guards at the gate and the thin, seedy-looking one standing near. Two more men, definitely Mexican, moved from in front of the square building as DeLora approached, and Fargo spotted two more men near a shed. "Open up," DeLora ordered, and one of the men lifted a heavy wooden latch bolt from the door. Fargo was beside Jessica as she followed DeLora into a large stone-walled space lighted by candles and kerosene lamps.

He saw Jessica's jaw grow tight as she saw the young women, each tied by an ankle iron with a chain that led to an iron peg set in the wall. Some wore torn slips, some wore only skirts, and a few wore only torn bloomers. Each sat or stood on a bed of straw with a water bowl nearby, and all looked up as DeLora entered, some with instant fright in their faces. "When they're cleaned up they're all good-looking," DeLora commented. Fargo's glance went to the two girls tethered side by side to one wall, apart from the others.

Their young, unlined faces already bore eyes that had lost hope. "Where'd you get them?" Jessica asked, and he saw she was having trouble keeping her voice even.

"That's my business. I get them from all over. The two young ones I got from a farmhouse where they happened to be alone. One of my lucky days," DeLora said and turned to Fargo. "You just want special stuff, take those two. I'll give you a good price. You'll be able to charge double, triple, for them—for a while, at least."

"What happens to the others if we don't take them?" Jessica asked, her voice tight and flat.

"I've some whorehouses in Mexico near Tijuana that'll take them," DeLora said. "They won't go to waste." Fargo cast a glance at Jessica and saw the tiny white spots on each cheekbone, the muscles of her long neck tight.

"I'm sure we can do business," Fargo said before Jessica's tensions burst. "But I'd still like to sleep on it. We'll come back tomorrow. Thanks for seeing us."

"Your call," Lucas DeLora said, and Fargo walked from the structure with him, watching his jowls shake with every step of his ample body. Outside, DeLora halted as Fargo and Jessica climbed onto the horses. "Don't wait too long. I might change my mind about doing business with you. I'm not happy about Carronna sending you to see me."

Fargo offered another broad smile. "I'll see if I can make it worth your while," he said, and DeLora watched him ride from the compound without an answering smile. Beyond the gate, Fargo kept the Ovaro at a slow trot with Jessica beside him as the dusk turned into night and he followed the trail of a half-moon to a tall sandstone pillar at the base of Superstition Mountain.

Only when he found a small cut did he halt and swing from the horse to turn to her. "What the hell were you doing back there? Trying to make DeLora close us out? Why'd you have to see the girls?" he flung at her.

"I wanted to see how many girls we have to save," Jessica retorted.

"We're not here to save any of them," Fargo said, and her eyes grew wide with shock.

"You can't mean that," she gasped.

"Did you see all the gunslingers he's got? We can't save those girls."

"We can't just leave them in the hands of that repulsive monster. You heard him say what he was going to do with them," Jessica said.

"I'm sorry, but we're here to do only one thing—save Moonrise. There's nothing else in the cards," Fargo said.

"Then why are you going back there?" she asked.

"I'm going to take another shot at finding out where he's sent Moonrise," Fargo said.

"And if that doesn't work?" she persisted.

"I'll back off on some pretext, wait till night, and try to take one of his gunslingers and find out what he can tell us."

"And if he tells you what you want to know?" Jessica pushed at him.

"We go after Moonrise. We've only got a matter of days. We found out that much," Fargo said.

"And leave all those girls to that bloodsucking pig," Jessica bit out.

"We can't do anything else, damn it. Bringing Moonrise back is what we have to do—that's first and foremost. I know it's a rotten, lousy hand, but that's the only one we have. We can't save those girls. It would only wreck any chance of our finding Moonrise." He tried to put a comforting hand on her shoulder but she pulled away.

"I guess I don't have your single-mindedness," she said, reproach in her voice.

"You're upset at what you've seen. You'll see I'm right when you've time to think about it," Fargo said gently.

"I doubt that." Jessica sniffed, took her bag, and went behind a rock to change. When she reappeared, wrapped in the sheet, she lay down, and he could feel her anger. He closed his eyes in sleep and decided to let time and the night calm her down.

When morning came and he woke and dressed, she was still made of silent, seething anger, unwilling to meet his eyes. She rode beside him in silence as he headed back to

Lucas DeLora's place. He broke the silence when they reached the gate.

"I'll do the talking from here on in," he told her, and she accepted the order in tight-lipped sullenness. The two rifle-toting guards at the gate admitted them, and Fargo reined to a halt and dismounted as DeLora's big bulk came to meet them. "I'd like another look at the girls," Fargo said, and DeLora led the way into the square structure with the seedy-looking man following. Inside, after glancing at the young women in their near-nakedness and ankle irons, Fargo turned to DeLora. "Can we talk alone?" he asked.

DeLora half shrugged. "Wait outside," he said to the other man, who left at once. DeLora studied Jessica with a long, frowning appraisal before returning his eyes to Fargo. "I'm getting the feeling we don't have much to talk about, mister," he said.

"Sure we do. That's why I want to talk alone. I thought you might feel more comfortable without outside ears. You see, I still want that Kiowa girl. I'll pay you to let me try to buy her from whoever has her. It'll be a deal just between us," Fargo said.

DeLora's brows lowered. "I told you she's sold. Forget about her, goddammit," he said.

"You'll get paid for just letting me try. Then I'll be back, win or lose, and take all these girls at your price. Now, I'd say that's a damn fair offer." Fargo smiled.

DeLora's fat face remained belligerent. "I say you're being a pain in the ass. Now, you take that high-toned little bitch and hightail it out of here and don't come back. I don't like the smell of this. I don't care if you take these bitches or not. I'll get rid of every damn one of them."

"No, you won't," Jessica's voice cut in, icy fury in it.

"What'd you say?" DeLora frowned, turning to her.

"I said you won't get rid of any of them, you rotten,

stinking monster," Jessica spit out, as with one quick motion she reached into the waist of her skirt. Her hand came out clutching a Remington four-barreled derringer with ivory grips. DeLora grabbed for his holster as he lunged at her, but Jessica fired all four barrels, one after the other. The four shots slammed into his fat frame at point-blank range and he halted, quivered as though he were a giant bowl of jam, and slowly collapsed, sinking to the floor in a heap.

"Jesus," Fargo swore as he saw Jessica drop the little pistol, drawing her hand back as though it were suddenly something horrible and unclean. Fargo spun, certain of what would happen next, and he was right. The door flew open and the tall, seedy figure entered, gun in hand. But Fargo had already drawn and the Colt barked. The figure flew backward out of the doorway and the door slammed shut. "The others will be coming," Fargo said, spinning on Jessica. "What the hell did you do that for?"

She straightened up, lifted her chin high. "So he wouldn't ever sell anyone else into slavery," she said. "I couldn't let him go on."

"And now how do we find Moonrise?" Fargo tossed at her, and she turned to DeLora's silent form.

"That's your problem," she said as she pushed her hand into the man's vest pocket.

"You should've let me work on it my way, then," Fargo snapped.

"I couldn't depend on your way," she said, continuing to go through DeLora's pockets. Finally she pulled out a set of keys and hurried to the nearest young woman, who wore only a skirt. She tried each of the keys and finally found the one that opened the ankle irons. The young woman stepped free, threw her arms around Jessica, and clung for a long moment. "I'll do the others. I'm Gracie," she said as she took the keys and Jessica stepped back.

"What'd he do with your clothes?" Jessica asked, and Gracie pointed to a large wooden box in a corner of the room as she began to free the other girls. Fargo returned his attention to the front door, where he heard the sounds of shouting and racing footsteps. He dropped to one knee, raised the Colt, and was ready when the door burst open. Three figures tried to rush in, firing wildly, but the Colt was already barking. Two of the figures fell at once, and the third flung himself sideways and rolled out of sight. Fargo took a long stride and kicked the door shut, slipped the latch bolt on, and reloaded. "That makes four, counting DeLora," he heard Jessica say.

"And that leaves at least four more," Fargo said. His eyes went to the young women, who were all free of the ankle irons now and tearfully hugging each other. One opened the box and began pulling out pieces of clothing. The two fifteen-year-olds pulled on blouses and came forward.

"We can't thank you enough, not really. We thought we were going to be used until they were through with us," the one said. "I'm Molly Haslipp and this is my cousin, Rhoda."

"Don't thank us. Nobody's home free yet. They've got us trapped. And the truth is, I didn't come here to save you," Fargo said with grim honesty.

"I know. I heard you with DeLora. You want to buy the Indian girl," Molly Haslipp said.

"Did you really come to do the same thing he was going to do to us?" her cousin asked.

"Please, we'll find a way to pay you back for letting us go," Gracie said, and Fargo saw the others looking on, fear again in their eyes.

"We're not here for that. Fargo just made up that story for DeLora," Jessica said.

"I didn't come to buy the Indian girl. I came to save her,"

Fargo said. "But now it looks like I may not be saving any-body." He tossed a hard glance at Jessica, who stayed wrapped in icy self-satisfaction. Fargo's words took on added meaning as a fusillade of shots slammed into the front door, splintering the latch bolt.

"You inside," a voice called out. "Send the girls out and we'll let you stay alive. We'll exchange you for the girls."

"If we say no?" Fargo called back.

"You all die together," another voice answered.

"Don't be stupid. We'll settle for the girls," the first voice called. Fargo's eyes went to the young women, who huddled together. They needed no words, their eyes saying the plea inside each. Fargo put a finger to his lips, a gesture of reassurance.

"Only if you tell me about the Indian girl. Where did he send her?" Fargo asked.

There was silence for a moment, and Fargo's ears picked up the whispered exchanges. "Tijuana," a voice called back, and Fargo saw Rhoda Haslipp step forward, her voice barely above a whisper.

"They're lying," she said. "I know about the man who bought her. DeLora offered me to him, too, but he only wanted the Indian girl," Rhoda Haslipp said.

"You know where he took her?" Fargo whispered back, and Rhoda nodded.

"A place called Puerto Penasco," she said.

"That's a port on the Gulf of California," Fargo breathed.

"His name's Lord Rothbury," Rhoda said.

"An Englishman. He's going to take her back to England. DeLora said he'd come a long way," Fargo murmured.

"We're not waitin' much longer, mister," the voice inter-rupted from outside the door.

"Come in after us if you're in such a hurry," Fargo an-swered.

"And have you pick us off as we come in? No, thanks. We figure you've enough water for another two days, tops. Then you'll have to come out and we'll do the picking off," the man said. "Give us the girls now and you can ride away."

"He's lying. They'll never let us go," Jessica said. "I say wait them out. Maybe they'll get tired and leave."

"We can't afford another three days. Moonrise could be on the Atlantic by then, if she isn't already," Fargo said. He bent down and picked up the derringer. "You have any more bullets for this thing?" he asked.

"One more round, four more," she said and fished into the pocket of her skirt.

"Load up," Fargo said, and when she had the little gun loaded he handed it to Rhoda. "You take this," he said, then drew the Colt from its holster and gave it to Molly. "You take this," he said. "Keep it hidden against your leg. Now put on the ankle irons again but don't lock them. That way you'll look like you're still wearing them but you'll be able to move and spin." He paused and searched Molly Haslipp's face, then her cousin's. "This is going to take two things to work. The first is surprise," he said.

"The other?" Molly asked.

"You being able to just shoot them down. You can't hesitate at the last moment. You can't have any last-minute qualms about it. Do you think you can do it?"

"Those rotten bastards. You can bet on it," Molly hissed.

"You'll shuffle out together in a line. Stay close to each other. I'll follow. They'll be mostly watching me. When you reach them you shoot. There are at least four of them. Take down as many as you can."

The young women nodded, faces grave as they slipped on the leg irons and lined up together. Fargo drew the thin-bladed, double-edged throwing knife from its calf holster and positioned it up his right sleeve. He stepped to the door, took a last glance back at the young women with Jessica at the end of the line. Their eyes told him they were ready. "You win. We're coming out. I'm sending the girls first," Fargo called through the door. The girls moved forward, Molly and Rhoda first in line. Fargo opened the door and stepped back to where Jessica waited. The young women shuffled out in their leg irons, one against the other, and Fargo followed with Jessica. His eyes swept DeLora's men and saw there were five. "You hit the ground at the first shot," he hissed at Jessica out of the corner of his mouth.

DeLora's men were staying close together, their eyes on him, Fargo saw with satisfaction. As the line of young women reached the spot where the men waited, Molly Haslipp in the lead, Rhoda right behind her, two of the men moved toward them. Arms at his sides, Fargo let the knife drop into his palm, his eyes on Molly Haslipp. He barely detected the faint movement of her right arm, but suddenly the shots split the air, instantly followed by the heavier report of the Colt firing. Three of the men went down almost in unison, and Fargo saw the fourth one yanking his gun from its holster. But Fargo's wrist had already flicked down and upward and the throwing knife hurtled through the air. The blade embedded itself in the base of the man's neck and his shot went wild. He clawed frantically at the hilt of the knife as he sank to his knees, then onto his side.

The fifth man had whirled and was racing to the stable. Fargo dug his heels into the ground and ran to where the Ovaro stood, reached the horse, and pulled the big Henry from its saddle case. He was bringing the rifle to his shoulder when the fifth man burst from the stable on a bay quarter horse that was already in a full gallop. Lowering the rifle, Fargo swung onto the Ovaro and took off after the fleeing figure. The man slowed only long enough to kick the gate open and then streaked across the flat, hard land. Fargo followed, the Ovaro quickly gaining, and the man sent his horse up an incline toward a line of rocks. He turned in the saddle to fire a shot that went far off its mark, and Fargo kept the pinto at a full gallop.

The Ovaro was closing distance quickly and the fleeing figure still had a good hundred yards to go before he reached the line of rocks. Fargo saw the man turn in the saddle, alarm on his face as he saw his pursuer closing in. He tried to shift directions, first to the right, then the left, plainly in an effort to make himself a more difficult target. It was his last mistake. All he did was lose more ground. Fargo raised the rifle to his shoulder as he stayed at a gallop. But as a rabbit senses a hawk about to pounce, the man felt the wings of death upon him and he whirled, emptying his six-gun in a hail of bullets. Fargo felt two of the bullets pass uncomfortably close, and he fired two shots from the big Henry. The man was swerving his horse again when he bucked in the saddle, his body quivering before it toppled from the horse, which kept running.

Fargo reined to a halt and stared down at the figure crumpled on the rocky soil. He slowly turned the Ovaro away, pushed the rifle into its saddle case, and rode back to DeLora's place. The women were waiting, and Rhoda handed him the Colt as he halted and swung to the ground. "Now we have to find a way to help you get to your homes," Jessica said.

"We don't have time for that," Fargo said.

"Well, we can find a wagon for them and stay with them until they're settled someplace," Jessica said.

"That'll all take time, too much time. We have to ride and ride hard," Fargo said as he retrieved the throwing knife.

"There are wagons DeLora used in the stable. We'll stay together and find our way back," Molly Haslipp said. "And I'm sure if we search the house we'll find more than enough money to get us wherever we want to go."

"I'm sure you will," Fargo said and waited as the young women exchanged hugs with Jessica.

"We've our lives back, thanks to you," Rhoda said and included Fargo in her glance.

"I'm glad for all of you," he said as he swung onto the Ovaro. "Hit the saddle," he snapped at Jessica, who pulled away from another hug and climbed onto the gelding. "Ride," he growled and put the horse into a fast canter. Jessica caught up with him a few hundred yards on and he shot her a quick, hard glance and saw the smugness in her face. "Satisfied with yourself, are you?" he barked.

"Yes," she returned. "It all worked out, didn't it?"

"No thanks to you, damn it," Fargo said.

"I'm the one who shot the rotten bastard," she said righteously.

"And when you did you wrecked any chance we had of finding out what happened to Moonrise. What Molly heard gave us another chance, nothing you did. Otherwise we'd have been lucky to get away alive, and we'd be at a dead end."

"We might still have saved the girls," Jessica countered.

"So you'd have saved ten people and condemned some forty to death. I don't think that squares off."

"That's a harsh, cruel way of seeing things," she protested.

"And this is a harsh, cruel land that takes harsh, cruel decisions," Fargo said.

"For you to make."

"That's right. You made a wrong one, and we managed

to luck out. Don't go patting yourself on the back," he said, and she glared at him as they rode on.

It wasn't until Fargo halted at a tiny trickle of a stream in the late afternoon that she spoke again.

"I don't have your kind of strength, and I don't know that I'd want to," she said.

He shrugged. "With some things, it's not what you want, it's what you are," he said, and he wondered if she'd let herself understand. It didn't much matter, he knew as they rode forward. She was going to get a lot angrier.

7

It was night when they reached Puerto Penasco and Fargo walked the horses down the waterfront streets. The gulf port was almost all waterfront, and with its apparently sizable amount of maritime traffic it sported three saloons instead of the usual one for a town its size, in addition to a bank and two rooming houses. The docks were lined with coastal vessels and some larger clipper ships. "We settle in first, then I'll go looking to find Lord Rothbury," Fargo said.

"How do you possibly expect to do that?" Jessica said, surveying the line of tall masts. "I'm sure he's kept a low profile."

"He made a special trip from England for Moonrise. I'll check out every English ship. There oughtn't be too many," Fargo said and drew up before a white-painted, clapboard building that proclaimed itself a waterfront inn.

"I'm hungry," Jessica said as they registered.

"I expect so. I didn't give us time to eat all day," Fargo said.

"There's a dining room to your left," the elderly desk clerk said. Fargo arranged for adjoining rooms and went into the small but neat dining room with Jessica, where they ordered antelope sandwiches.

"You surprise me," she said. "I expected you'd insist on

searching the waterfront first. The ship you want could be sailing out under your nose."

"I don't want you fainting from lack of food," he said.

"An attack of charitableness. I'm touched," she said.

"Good," he said. "Besides, there won't be any ships sailing till after midnight. I checked the tide. It's too low to sail."

"Damn you, Fargo. I might've known," she hissed and bit into her sandwich.

"You wouldn't want me to change character," he said, and she refused to answer. When the meal ended he went out to the horses while Jessica went to her room. He returned, carrying his lariat, and knocked on her door.

"What's that for?" she asked when she let him in.

He offered a genial smile and spun her with quick, sharp motions that took but seconds to bring her arms behind her and encircle her wrists with a length of the lariat. "Sorry to be so sudden," he said.

"What are you doing? What is this?" Jessica frowned and tried to pull her arms free, but he tightened the rope and she gave a little yelp. He severed the wrist ropes with his knife and pushed Jessica into a chair, where he had another length of rope around her instantly. "Let me go. What do you think you're doing?" she flung at him.

"You've a role to play, Jessica. I'm going to see that you play it without arguments and without bone-headed stunts," Fargo said as he finished tying her to the chair.

"You untie me this instant," she demanded.

"Sorry," he said and tied her ankles, then produced a kerchief, which he put over her mouth and tied firmly in place. He examined the gag when he finished. "You'll be able to breathe without any trouble," he said, and the fury in her eyes visually translated the muffled mumblings beneath the gag. "Don't waste your energy trying to get loose. You can't," he said. "I'll be back." He strode to the door, glancing over his shoulder to see her pulling and tugging to get loose. He'd expected that and closed the door after him as he left the room and hurried down the hallway.

Outside, he strode through the night to the docks, where he peered at every ship as he made his way along the waterfront. He was almost at the last dock when he halted before a two-masted staysail schooner. His eyes hung on the home port inscription beneath the vessel's name: LONDON. He strolled onto the gangplank and reached the top before a seaman accosted him. "Hold it there, mate," the man said.

"I'm looking for Lord Rothbury," Fargo said.

"Wait right there," the sailor said and hurried across the deck to a center cabin. *Bull's-eye*, Fargo thought to himself as two other seamen came up to stand guard. The first seaman returned in a few minutes, accompanied by a tall man wearing an expensive frock coat and tailor-made trousers, a ruffled shirt, and ruffled cuffs. Fargo took in a face that would have been ascetic were it not for fleshy, sensuous lips and weakness where there should have been strength. The figure halted and peered at Fargo out of light blue eyes, framed by curly, carefully combed brown hair that hung to the shirt collar.

"I don't know you, my good man," Lord Rothbury said in a clipped British accent.

"You don't, but we have a mutual friend. Lucas DeLora," Fargo said. "Or, I should say we had."

"Had?" the man echoed, tilting his head.

"DeLora's dead, killed in a gunfight," Fargo said.

"Did you have anything to do with it?" the Englishman asked.

"No," Fargo said. "In fact, I was lucky enough to get your name from him before it happened. I came to him to buy that Kiowa girl, and now I hope I can buy her from you."

"I see," the man murmured, still studying Fargo.

"Is there somewhere else we can talk?" Fargo asked.

"This way," Lord Rothbury said, and Fargo followed him to the ship's cabin, down a short companionway and into a large cabin well outfitted with table and side settees. Another man rose from one of the settees. He was portly, gray-haired, with spectacles, and equally well dressed in the clothes of a proper English gentleman. "This is my personal physician, Dr. Allwin," Rothbury said. "I didn't get your name, sir."

"Fargo . . . Skye Fargo," the Trailsman answered and cast a glance at the other man. "You always travel with your doctor?" he asked.

"No, I'm quite healthy." The man smiled tolerantly. "I bring Dr. Allwin along to be sure I'm not being cheated."

Fargo considered the answer for a moment and then allowed a slow smile. "Such as paying for a virgin and not getting one?"

"Precisely," Rothbury said. "I'm afraid I always felt that Mr. DeLora wouldn't hesitate to cheat anyone. I wanted to make certain that wouldn't happen to me. I insisted on Dr. Allwin's examining the goods offered."

"Very smart," Fargo said.

"Now, as for the Indian girl, I'm afraid she's not for sale. I came all the way here from London for her. I'd written to DeLora about finding someone really special. You see, I head an exclusive gentleman's club in London. We've made it into a quite elegant pastime, indulging only in the services of very special, very different young women. They must all start as virgins. That's one of our conditions. We hold a raffle to see which of our members wins the honor of being first in line, raise quite a bit of money for various charities. Of course, they've no idea where our donations come from, which amuses us."

"I suppose all the members are fine gentlemen such as yourselves," Fargo said, including the doctor in his glance.

"Indeed," Rothbury said. "So you see, buying the Kiowa girl is pretty much out of the question. She fills our requirements for the special and the different."

"Only I didn't come empty-handed. Fact is, I brought you something much better, more appealing to your gentlemen. The Kiowa girl won't be anything much once you wear the bloom off her. She'll never be the kind who'll appeal to your members over the long haul. I've got that kind of girl for you, the niece of a United States senator."

Fargo watched as Lord Rothbury's lips pursed and interest slid across his ascetic countenance. "The niece of a United States senator?" he said slowly. "Now, that is interesting."

"Thought you'd like that," Fargo said.

"And you have her with you?" Rothbury questioned. Fargo nodded. "She has to be a virgin, you understand. That's one of our requisites," the man added.

"She is. She's a little spitfire, but I'm sure you have your ways of bringing your girls into line," Fargo said.

"We do. They learn their world has changed and they'd better make the best of it," the man said.

"Can we do business?" Fargo asked.

"If she measures up. I'll look at her. That's as far as I'll go, now. To use one of your American expressions, I won't buy a pig in a poke," Rothbury said, and the doctor chuckled. "Can you bring her? I'd like to sail by morning," Rothbury said.

"I'll be back," Fargo said. "But I'd like to see the Indian girl. I don't buy any pigs in pokes, either."

"She's still not for sale as of this moment, but I don't see why you can't have a look at her," Rothbury said and motioned to Dr. Allwin. "Come along, old boy?"

"Why not?" the physician said, and Fargo followed as he was led back onto the deck, to the stern of the vessel, where he went down a steep companionway into the stern hold. Rothbury opened the door and Fargo followed into the interior of the ship's hold where a lamp lighted the area. Fargo saw the slender figure stand up, chains around one ankle, and he took in jet-black hair, black eyes, high cheekbones, and a straight nose—a handsome, strong face. She looked at her visitors with the regal bearing befitting a chief's daughter, only contempt in the black eyes. Moonrise wore an elkhide dress, instantly defined as Kiowan by the irregular cut at the bottom portion of the cape. High breasts pushed the top of the garment outward and he glimpsed strong, shapely calves.

"Very handsome," Fargo said.

"Yes, and she's been taught enough English to speak quite well. She is special, just what our members will enjoy," Rothbury said.

"They don't wear well, not for your kind of membership," Fargo said. "I've something better. I'll be back within a half hour." He turned, his eyes seemingly casual as he glanced around the ship's hold. Lord Rothbury followed him onto the deck. Fargo paused, surprised as heavy strands of fog suddenly rolled in over the ship and the waterfront.

"Damn," Rothbury said. "I hope this won't delay our sailing. These coastal fogs of yours are as bad as anything we have in England." He watched as Fargo hurried down the gangplank and disappeared into the fog that had grown heavy with astonishing speed. Hurrying to the inn he went to Jessica's room and saw that she had managed to scoot her chair across the floor, where she was wedged against the wall in helpless fury. Her eyes shot rage at him as he undid her ankles first, then the rope binding her to the chair, and lifted her to her feet. He explained nothing to her. He knew what she had already concluded and he wanted it left that way.

It had its cruelty, but he couldn't help that. She wasn't a good enough actress to put on a performance that would fool Rothbury and the doctor. He wanted her fury and her fear to be real—unmistakably real. Ignoring the sounds from underneath the gag, he took her from the room and out a rear entrance to the street. Between the lateness of the hour and the fog that had grown thicker, he saw no one on the waterfront streets. Holding tightly to her, he peered through the fog at the prows of the ships that now seemed ghostly apparitions that materialized and faded away. Finally, he found the schooner and led Jessica onto the vessel, where two seamen confronted him at once.

"Lord Rothbury's waiting for us," Fargo said. One of the men disappeared, returning in moments and leading the way across the now fog-shrouded deck to the cabin amidships. A shaft of yellow light reached out into the fog, and Fargo saw Rothbury waiting in the doorway. Fargo pushed Jessica into the cabin and Rothbury closed the door. His eyes quickly appraised the full beauty of Jessica, Fargo saw, lingering on the corn-silk hair. Fargo took the gag away from Jessica's mouth and she shot daggers at him with her dark blue eyes.

"You bastard," she hissed.

"I told you she was high-spirited," Fargo said with a smile.

"But very beautiful, I must say," Rothbury said.

"Indeed," the doctor agreed.

Rothbury circled Jessica as she aimed a kick at Fargo but missed. He caught her before she fell. "You let me go, damn you," Jessica spit at him. "You can't do this. You can't. It's not fair."

"I like all that fire," Rothbury said. "She'll be quite something even when she's brought into line."

"I knew you'd see that," Fargo said. The man's ascetic face almost quivered as he continued to circle Jessica. Fargo felt the rage inside himself. The man was a stinking toad, a miserable sadist—regardless of his fine manners and wealthy background. Fargo wanted to smash his arrogant face in, but he knew this wasn't the time.

"All that fire is missing with the Indian girl," the doctor put in. "We talked about that, remember?"

"Yes, I do, Allwin. And I'm bothered by that. She's all stoicism and no passion," Rothbury said.

"That's the way they are," Fargo said, happy to feed into the man's lack of knowledge about the Indian. Jessica's voice broke into his thoughts.

"You can't do this, Fargo. This makes you no better than that pig, DeLora," she accused.

He ignored her as Rothbury turned to him. "You say she's a virgin," Rothbury said. "Then you won't mind if I have Dr. Allwin verify that."

"Be my guest," Fargo said.

"What?" Jessica screamed at him. "You can't. You wouldn't."

"It's just an examination. It won't hurt you," Fargo said with a shrug. Jessica lunged at him again and tried to sink her teeth into his arm, but he sidestepped the attempt.

"Let's get two of the men to hold her for you," Rothbury said and stepped from the cabin with the physician following him.

"I better be right about you or the devil's out the window," Fargo mused aloud.

"You stinking bastard. I'll kill you. I will, I will," she

cried out, her voice breaking as she aimed another kick at him and tried to run. He grabbed her and pushed her against the cabin wall as Rothbury, the doctor, and two crewmen entered.

"Into my cabin with her," the doctor said, and the two men carried Jessica away kicking and screaming. Fargo winced inwardly but kept his face casually expressionless as he heard her screams and curses through the closed door of the adjoining cabin.

"Why do you want the Kiowa girl over this beautiful little spitfire, Fargo?" Rothbury asked as they waited. It was the question he'd expected would come and he was ready for it.

"I don't know if I can make you understand, but she'll be special to some of my clients in a way she never would to your gentlemen," he said. "You could say it hangs on history, cultural and social heritage, all the attitudes that'll make a lot of people real happy to enjoy an Indian girl."

"Yes, I can understand that," Rothbury said as the door opened and Jessica came from the adjoining cabin, the doctor holding her by one arm.

"Absolutely, milord," the doctor said with more glee than professionalism in his voice. Fargo met Jessica's eyes. She peered at him with a mixture of incomprehension, defeat, and bitterness. He wanted to offer comfort but knew he didn't dare. Lord Rothbury turned to him, his thin lips pursed.

"I've a proposition for you, my dear fellow," he began. "I paid a lot of money for the Indian girl. I'm not able to spend for another girl, even one as perfect for us as yours. Therefore, I propose an exchange. I'll take her and give you the Indian girl."

Fargo let himself frown in thought. "The niece of a

United States senator for a Kiowa girl? Hardly seems a fair exchange," he said.

"Look, you really want the Indian girl. You made that quite clear, and you brought Jessica to sell. An exchange seems quite in order, I'd say," Rothbury countered.

"Maybe you're right," Fargo conceded and added a touch of magnanimity. "We've a deal. I'll take the girl now."

"Yes," Rothbury said. "I want to sail come morning if the damn fog permits." He ordered the two seamen to take Jessica to the stern hold, went along, and Fargo followed. Inside the hold, an ankle chain was put on Jessica and attached to a peg against the ship's wall. She turned to him and he saw defeat in the dark blue orbs.

"You're getting your way, and I hate you. I'll never forget this. I know what you're doing. One life . . . mine . . . against forty others. But you've no right to make these decisions. You've no right to play God, no right at all," she said.

"Life's full of things that aren't right," he said. "But sometimes they work out."

"Trying to make yourself feel better?" she threw at him, her bitterness corroding. He turned away and cursed silently as he went to where the seamen had freed Moonrise. He took her by the arm, his voice a whisper.

"Hear me, Moonrise," he said.

Her eyes grew wide at once. "You know my name. I never tell them," she whispered back.

"Your father told me," Fargo breathed and saw her eyes grow still wider and search his face. But she said nothing more, her understanding incomplete. "We'll talk later," he said, and she went with him quietly as he climbed the gangplank when Rothbury came up, the doctor in tow.

"Perhaps we'll do business again, Fargo. You might take Lucas DeLora's place as my supplier," Rothbury said.

"Maybe," Fargo said and hurried down the gangplank as the two men were quickly swallowed up by the fog, which blanketed the waterfront now. He made his way through the streets, peering through the fog as it drifted in an erratic pattern. When he found the inn he took Moonrise to the room and took his hand from her arm. She turned to face him, black eyes again searching his face.

"Why did my father tell you my name?" she asked.

"Because he sent me to find you," Fargo said.

"Then you must be a great tracker," she said.

"They call me the Trailsman. It is what I do," he said.

"My father would not call on you if you were not a great among the great," she said.

"You will stay here, now, until I come back," he said.

"I have nowhere to run," she said.

"That is not enough," he said.

"I give you my word as a Kiowa chief's daughter," she said. "And as a woman you have saved."

"That'll do," he said and spun as he hurried from the room. Outside, the fog continued to roll in, and he peered through the dampness as he made his way back to the ship. He started up the gangplank and dropped to one knee as the voices came to him, Rothbury's first.

"This vessel is under my charter. I say we put out at once, fog or no fog," the man said.

"Charter or no charter, I'm still the captain of this ship," the second voice said. "I won't put out in a fog. We could run aground five minutes after we leave. Besides, there's not enough bloody wind to set sail."

Fargo heard Rothbury utter a curse and the sound of his footsteps fading as he strode back to his cabin. Fargo moved forward in a crouch, pushed his way through the fog, then shrunk against the side of the vessel as two shadowy forms materialized and then melted away. He found the stern hold and noiselessly pulled the door open. He was down the companionway and into the hold on silent feet. Jessica looked up in the relatively fog-free interior. Her mouth dropped open as she stared at him.

He held a finger to his lips as he reached her in three long strides. Astonishment whirled through her face. "Proof you should never jump to conclusions," he whispered, cursing as he examined the ankle chain and the wall peg. He glanced around the hold to find a tool to open the chain lock and saw nothing. Voices from the deck sounded—Rothbury again.

"You've emergency oars aboard," the man said. "Cast off and row the damn ship. I've a feeling that bastard may come back. I want to be away from the dock before he does."

"Your responsibility, milord," the captain's voice answered.

Fargo drew his lips back as he pulled the Colt from its holster and placed the muzzle across Jessica's ankle and against the chain. "There's no other way. Hold still and get ready to run like hell," he said. He steadied the gun, slowly pulled back on the trigger, and fired, the explosion tremendous in the confines of the hold. But the lock shattered and he yanked the remainder of the chain free from Jessica as she pushed to her feet. The shouts from the deck were equally instant. She was at his heels as he bounded up the companionway and onto the stern deck. A seaman loomed up in front of him, and Fargo brought the pistol around in a short arc. It smashed into the man's temple and he went down.

Footsteps pounded through the fog, and two more figures materialized. Fargo glimpsed the long, thin shape of a rifle in one man's hands, brought the Colt up again, and fired two shots. Both figures seemed to dissolve in the fog as they disappeared. "This way," he hissed at Jessica as he ran down the deck and heard Rothbury's voice.

"I was right, goddammit," the man said. "It's him. It has to be." A bank of fog rolled in, obscuring everything. Fargo slowed, put one hand on the rail and felt his way, stumbled and fell to one knee. But they had found the gangplank, and he pulled himself to his feet as the fog suddenly lightened in the erratic way of fogs. He whirled and saw Rothbury, a heavy pistol in his hand, the doctor's shorter figure behind him.

"Run," Fargo said and pushed Jessica down the gangplank as he dived to the deck. Rothbury's shot went over his head and he rolled behind a winch as the men ran forward, pistols still raised. Fargo lifted the Colt just as another trail of fog swept in, and he fired as Rothbury disappeared and knew his shot had missed. But he heard the man moving to come up behind him, circling the winch, and he turned, letting his ears become his eyes. Rothbury was close, very close, and Fargo dropped to one knee as he peered into the fog. Suddenly, the fog drew apart, a curtain shredding, and Rothbury was directly in front of him, hardly more than two feet away, his pistol raised. He fired, but Fargo managed to dive and let the shot pass over his head. He slammed into the man's ankles, wrapped both arms around his legs, and Rothbury went down backward. The back of his head slammed into a steel hook that held the bottom of two rigging blocks onto the main rail.

Fargo heard the crack of the hook driving through flesh and bone, and Rothbury's figure went limp. Fargo lifted the man by the legs, upended him, and flung him over the side of the rail. The splash sounded as Fargo spun to see Dr. Allwin there, fear on the physician's round face. "He won't be coming up," Fargo growled, the Colt aimed at the doctor. Four men came up, appearing through the fog, and

Fargo reached out and yanked the doctor to him, pressing the Colt against the man's temple.

"No, no, please, I didn't have anything to do with it. I was just brought along," the man whimpered as the crewmen halted.

"Bullshit, Doc. You were part of his little club, cut out of the same cloth," Fargo said.

"Please, none of it was my doing," the man almost sobbed.

"Shut up," Fargo snapped. "Tell them to get back."

"Do as he says," Allwin ordered, his voice quavering, and the men retreated to melt into the fog.

"I'm going to do you a favor, because I want you to take a message back to your friends in jolly old London," Fargo said. "Tell them never, never, never to come back here again to stock their fancy whorehouses. If they do, I'll get on a boat and come looking for you. Understand?"

"Yes, indeed, very clearly. We won't be coming back. Depend on it," the doctor said shakily. Fargo pulled the Colt back and flung the portly figure across the deck, where he went sprawling into the fog. Spinning, Fargo raced down the gangplank and leaped onto the dock.

"Over here," Jessica's voice called, and he peered into the fog and saw her come toward him.

"Let's go," he said.

"I want to talk," she said. "About this."

"Later," he said, took her hand, and pulled her with him along the waterfront. He found the inn and brought her to the room, where Moonrise stood up as they entered. Her black eyes went to Jessica, then held on Fargo.

"You save her, too," Moonrise said. "You are great warrior and great tracker. I know now why my father calls on you."

"He didn't exactly call," Fargo said wryly.

"But he knew about you," Moonrise said.

"He did," Fargo nodded and opened the door to the adjoining room. "You will sleep here. We wait till morning to ride," he said.

Moonrise returned a single nod, her handsome face unsmiling. "I will sleep hard for the first time in many moons," she said. "It will be a good thing."

"Good," he said and closed the door after her when she stepped into the next room. He turned to see Jessica's eyes studying him, a small furrow creasing her brow. Her voice was more reproachful than accusing.

"Why didn't you tell me what you planned? Why didn't you tell me you intended to come back for me?" she said.

"No, thanks," he said. "You might've pulled another Carronna with that temper of yours. This time we mightn't have been so lucky."

"Is that all?"

"No. You couldn't have pulled it off. You know you wouldn't have gone along with the good doctor. You had to be just what you were, a prisoner who hated everything about me and what I was doing."

She said nothing, but he saw the reluctant understanding in her face. She stepped forward, put her palms against his chest. "I'm sorry for the things I said. I'm sorry I didn't trust you," she murmured, and her arms came up to slide around his neck. "I'm grateful, terribly, terribly grateful." Her lips touched his cheek, lingered, and her arms tightened around his neck. Her breath was suddenly a thing of tiny gasps. But he didn't move and she stepped back and brought her arms down. "Sorry," she said. "I forgot for a moment."

"Forgot what?" he asked.

"About your preferences in women," she said and started to turn away. But he pulled her back and his mouth closed on hers. He felt her stiffen for a moment, surprise in her eyes, and then her lips softened and her eyes closed. He pressed harder, his lips opening her mouth, his tongue edging out to just touch her lips.

"Oh," she murmured. "Oh." His hand caressed her neck, moved down to her collarbone, pressed further, and the top of her blouse opened. He moved her backward, to the bed against the far wall of the room, and she lay back with him. "No—I mean, what are you doing?" she muttered. His mouth pressed hers, hungrily now, his tongue darting forward and back, tiny harbingers of motion and pleasure.

"Don't you know?" he asked.

"Yes, oh, God, yes. Be careful . . . oh, please," Jessica said.

His hand moved further and the blouse came open entirely, sliding from her shoulders, and he took in the creamy white breasts, enticingly filled out at the cups, each tipped by a delicately pink, smooth nipple, beautifully virginal, on an equally delicate small pink circle. His thumb rubbed gently across first one tip and then the other, and Jessica uttered a tight little cry and her hands clutched at his arms. He shed shirt then trousers as his lips closed around one breast, pulled gently, and Jessica gasped, pure pleasure in the sound. He undid her skirt, pulled, and it came off, along with her half-slip. He saw a lovely narrow waist, a lean yet well-covered body, ribs only barely showing, a flat abdomen, and small, slightly convex little belly with a perfectly round indentation in the center.

Her hips were lean yet wide, appealingly inviting, and he enjoyed the small but thick triangle, and below it, thighs that were magnificently long and smooth. His hand moved gently down her body and her hips quivered and her legs drew up together, pressed tightly against each other and fell from side to side as one. "My God, oh, God, oh . . . aaaaah,"

Jessica murmured as his mouth caressed her breasts, then moved down to nibble along her body, across her belly, pausing to push into the round little indentation. "I've never . . . I've never . . ." she breathed, and stopped, and her hand came down to grasp his, pushing it downward. "Yes, yes, oh, God . . . oh, yes," she cried out and drew her hand back only when he pushed into the thick triangle and pressed against a very round, swollen pubic mound. He rested a moment there, let the wanting inside her spiral, finally moved downward again and felt the moistness at the bottom of the triangle. Jessica let out a hoarse cry as his hand slid further, between her still tightly pressed together thighs, touched the wetness of her. Suddenly her legs fell open, closed, opened again, twisted, stayed open, twisted again.

"Yes, yes, Jesus, yes," she cried out, and now her body twisted from side to side and he saw the creamy, longish breasts falling to the right, then the left, and he pressed his mouth to one as his hand cupped the wet portal. "Oh, my God, oh, my God," she half screamed, and he moved his hand upward, his fingers gently caressing, touching the velvet liquidity of her inner lips. Jessica's hips leaped upward with a sudden explosion and fell back again, leaped and fell back. He brought his own throbbing erectness against her, pushed through the dense nap, and Jessica's fists pounded against his back. "Take me . . . oh, my God, take me . . . oh, oh . . . ooooohhh," she panted, pleaded, and knew the ecstasy of the flesh, the ultimate discovery of the body, desire sublimating all else.

He moved slowly, sliding forward into her lubricious tunnel, and felt the tightness of her, paused, and Jessica screamed in protest and clawed his back. "Don't stop, please don't stop," she said, and he saw her lips were pulled back in a kind of smile, her mouth open, every part of her focused on the fulfillment of ecstasy. He moved again, deeper, and felt the tightness of her give way, flesh summoning flesh, desire calling on desire, senses spiraling to places never reached before, sensuous goals only imagined and now given freedom. Jessica uttered a deep sigh and surged her hips forward, meeting his slow thrust, engulfing him, absorbing his gift to her, giving and possessing. "Ah . . . ah, yes, ah, good . . . ah, so good," Jessica cried out, and she surged again with him, rose, smooth thighs lifting, clasping themselves to him.

He felt the tightening inside her, slow coils, growing, spiraling, and she flung her torso from one side to the other, breasts falling right, then left, her hands little fists pounding into the bed, all sensation beyond control, all pleasure edging the endurance of ecstasy. Suddenly her hands opened, grasped hold of the bedsheet, twisted and pulled as she began to quiver. "My God, my God, oh, yes, yes, yes . . . now, now, oh, now, oh, God, I can't stand it . . . I can't—" she half screamed as she clutched him to her. He felt himself pulsating inside her, sweeping away all else, and he exploded with her. Jessica screamed into his chest, bit his skin, pulled on him, clung so tightly it was as if she wanted to become one with him, ecstasies intertwining, flesh fusing into one pinnacle of pleasure.

But finally she stopped quivering, clinging, vibrating, and she fell back onto the bed as a deep groan of protest engulfed her. "Oh, no, no . . . more, I want more . . ." she gasped, and he brought his mouth to one creamy mound, held it there, gently enveloped the tiny pink tip. Slowly, her gasps grew softer, longer, became little sighs that mixed contentment with reluctant acceptance. Finally, he drew his mouth from her and she gave a tiny cry. "So much . . . so much . . . more than I ever imagined," she whispered and nestled against him. She fell into a half sleep, in a world unto herself and he lay with her, one leg draped across the damp triangle.

Time became a thing without beginning or end, a sweet oasis of satisfaction, until finally he felt her stir and push up onto her elbows. He drew his leg back and she sat up, longish breasts swaying beautifully, but he saw the tiny frown that had dug itself into her forehead as she studied him. "Why all of a sudden? What happened to your taste in women?" she asked.

"Guess it just changed," he said.

Her frown dug deeper. "No, it didn't just change all of a sudden. You didn't respond at all those other moments. You very definitely turned away," she said, and he saw her lips tightening. "You did it on purpose, didn't you? You purposely didn't let anything happen. You turned away because you wanted me to be a virgin when the time came. You planned the whole thing out."

"Planning means the difference between winning and losing," he said as she glared at him.

"You bastard. You let me feel I wasn't attractive enough," Jessica hissed.

"It was damn hard to pull off," he said, cupped her breasts in his hands, and pulled her to him.

"Bastard," she sighed as her mouth opened on his. "You're going to make up for that."

"With pleasure," he said as she curled herself around him. It was a demand he knew he'd enjoy.

8

He made a good start at obeying her demand, yet managed to get some sleep by the time the new day dawned. Jessica stirred lazily as he swung from the bed, her smooth, long body a newly awakened monument to pleasure. She opened her eyes as he pulled her to a sitting position. "Time out for unfinished business, remember?" he said, and she nodded and swung her long legs from the bed. Fargo dressed first and opened the door to the adjoining room. He stepped inside to see Moonrise sitting up in bed, beautifully naked, small but high breasts erect, each tipped with a dark pink nipple on a darker circle. A narrow waist tapered down to a flat abdomen and a small triangle that was little more than soft fuzz.

Her black eyes met his gaze with quiet pride and he thought he saw the hint of a smile. "I am happy to see you, Fargo," she said, unfolded nicely shaped legs, and stood up. Her beauty was made of both delicacy and strength.

"You sleep well?" Fargo asked.

"Yes. I am ready to go back," Moonrise said.

"I think you'd better dress first," Fargo said.

"I wanted you to see what can be yours," she said. "It is the way of my people to give to those who give to us. I have only myself to give."

"I am honored by such a gift," Fargo said, responding in

what he knew was the proper way to respond. But the voice that answered came from behind him.

"How nice," it said crisply, and he saw Jessica step into the room, tightening her skirt. She moved to face Moonrise. "I'm Jessica," she said firmly.

"Jess-ee-ka," Moonrise repeated.

Jessica nodded and turned to Fargo. "Tell her I'll do all the giving around here," she said.

"We get possessive pretty damn quick," Fargo commented.

"We don't share some things," Jessica said tartly, spun on her heel, and returned to the other room.

"She is Fargo's woman," Moonrise said.

He nodded. For now, he thought to himself. Moonrise half shrugged and pulled the elkskin dress over herself. She followed Fargo into the other room. "She'll ride with me," he said to Jessica.

"I don't care who she rides with. I care who she sleeps with," Jessica said. Fargo waited until Moonrise came from the other room before going outside. Shreds of the fog still clung, but most of it had already dissipated. Fargo swung onto the Ovaro and took Moonrise to ride in front of him. Jessica stayed alongside as he rode from the port, turned north, and set a hard pace until he stopped for water in the late afternoon at a small *tinaja*. Jessica knelt to fill her canteen beside him, corn-silk hair glistening in the sun. "What happens tonight?" she asked.

"We sleep," Fargo answered. "Close together."

Her eyes held on him. "I'd hoped for something else," she said.

"Not till this is over," he said.

"Why? Afraid of her knowing?" Jessica said.

"In a way," he said.

"You want to explain more?"

"She offered me a gift. I didn't take it. To the Indian, that could be taken as an insult. She's choosing not to take it that way. Sleeping with you in front of her would be a mark of disrespect after her offer. I don't want that. I want to be on good terms with her until we get back," Fargo said.

"Is that important?"

"It might be. I'm not taking any chances," he said, and he saw disappointment mingle with acceptance in her face. "I'll see to it that you'll be too tired to think of anything but sleep," he said.

"Want to bet?" she tossed back and returned to her horse.

He rode on, Moonrise sitting with him in silence as he set a hard pace. They bedded down only when the moon was high. She slept naked on the elkskin dress, and Jessica stayed on her sheet in exhaustion. When morning came, he set the same grueling pace, circling across the hard, dry land whenever he spotted signs of Apache. He kept to the pace each day, and at night they all slept the sleep of the exhausted. But he made good time, and gradually the land began to change its face, the harsh rock and dryness giving way to good soil and buffalo grass, the bristlebrush and paloverde bowing to bluestem and bur oak.

"You ride hard like Kiowa warrior, Fargo," Moonrise said near the close of one day, and he nodded at the compliment. He saw the strain in Jessica's face, but there was no time to slow, and he set another day of blistering pace, halting when the night was deep. He had undressed to his underdrawers when Jessica came to him.

"We're getting close," she said. "I notice the change in the trees and the soil."

"Very good," he said.

"And I haven't forgotten why I came here in the first place. I want you to ask her about my uncle. Maybe she knows something," Jessica said.

He thought for a moment and found no harm in agreeing. He went to where Moonrise had just shed her dress. She looked handsome and beautiful and completely calm. "I came here for Jessica, to seek a man," he said. "Tall, taller than I am, hair like moonlight snow, thin as a new tree. He walked with one bad leg."

Her eyes narrowed a fraction. "Yes," she said. "He and five others. They were caught." She drew her arm back as if she were drawing a bow and firing an arrow.

"Dead? All?" Fargo questioned and she nodded. He grunted and went back to where Jessica sat wrapped in the sheet. "Your search is over," he said gently.

Jessica stared back for a long moment and then looked away. "I kept hoping," she said. "I hate this land. It's nothing but cruelty and savagery." He nodded and wanted to tell her that there was more, another side to it, but they would have been words falling on deaf ears so he stayed silent. He heard her sobbing softly before she lapsed into sleep, and when morning came the sadness was in her eyes. He rode hard again, the land growing familiar. It was midday when Moonrise spoke.

"Stop," she said. He reined to a halt and she turned in the saddle to look at him. "I think one more day," she said.

"Yes," he said.

"We must talk," she said and slid to the ground. He dismounted as she faced him, her handsome face grave. "How many of your people does my father hold?" she asked.

Fargo felt his jaw drop in surprise. "How did you know?" he frowned.

"I know my father. I know his ways. He would not trust you to keep your word," she said simply.

Fargo made a grim sound. "Many, too many," he said.

Moonrise thought for a moment, and then her black eyes searched his face again. "You have not taken the gift I offered, because of her," she said with a gesture to Jessica. "But you found me, you saved me, you do this, and I must give you something. For my own honor, I must do that, so I tell you this. Red Hawk will not let your people go when you bring me back. He will kill them and he will kill you."

Fargo stared in disbelief at her. "We made a bargain. He gave his word."

The girl's expression didn't change. "But that is what he will do. I know my father," she said.

"That would not be the way of a Kiowa chief. It would bring dishonor to him and to his word," Fargo said.

"His word is good only to those he honors."

"And that's not me," Fargo frowned.

"It is no white man, no one who sits with the bluecoats," Moonrise said.

"He hates that much?" Fargo inquired. "Why?"

"I had a brother, grown up when I was born. Soldiers wanted to ask him about a raid. Only talk, only questions, they said. He went to meet then with eight others. All were shot down. There was never any talk. It was a trick. Red Hawk ate the seeds of hate that day. He said no mercy ever, no honor ever."

"He used me. He never intended to keep the bargain," Fargo said.

"There was never a bargain. There was only bringing me back. He chose well. He is a great chief, my father."

"He's a son of a bitch," Fargo threw back.

The hint of a smile touched her finely etched lips. "You are the same in many ways," she said, and Fargo's frown was indignant protest. "Nothing stopped you from finding me. You did whatever you had to do. The Kiowa say, the eagle never loses sight of its prey, the arrow never changes course. My father never loses sight of his hate. The eagle and the arrow. You are much the same."

He shrugged away her words, unwilling to entertain her insights. "Thank you for what you've told me," he said. "You have paid your debt. Now we ride again." He swung onto the pinto and she came with him. Jessica had halted a half-dozen yards away, and he saw the curiosity in her face as he passed her. He rode with thoughts spinning through him. It was all different, all very changed, and new dangers had become a whirlwind. He hadn't come all this way, and done all he had, to let it end in betrayal and death. Yet the forty prisoners were suddenly much closer to death than they'd been when he left. The irony of it stabbed at him. He had to return Moonrise to save their lives, yet in returning her they would die. They had ridden another hour when he spoke to her. "You know, I cannot let this happen," he said.

"You will do whatever you must. My father will do whatever he must," she said.

"And you?"

"I will do whatever I must."

He uttered a wry sound. She had pulled together the thoughts that had whirled through his mind, and it was all coming down to a final, strange end where perhaps only that grim irony would be the final victor. He rode for only another hour, then pulled to a halt under a stand of cottonwoods. "Extra sleep tonight," he said. "No riding till midnight."

"That's the most welcome thing I've heard since we started back," Jessica said as dusk began to slide over the land. He saw Moonrise find a spot for herself beside a gnarled trunk and he sat down and watched Jessica change into her sheet and lie down a half-dozen yards away. He waited till she slept, hardly more than a few minutes' wait, then he rose and took his lariat from the Ovaro. He walked toward Moonrise, and she sat up as she saw him approach. She offered a wry smile.

"I wondered," she said.

"We are too close. You could find your way from here," he said. "You are a Kiowa."

"You don't want that. It could destroy your plans," she said.

"I don't have any plans yet," he said. It was only a half lie. He was furiously searching for a plan, turning options in his mind, few as they were. "But I will bring you back on my terms, not on his, not on yours," he said.

She extended her wrists for him to tie. "I think it would have been good, very good," she said, and his eyes questioned. "If you had accepted my first offer," she explained.

"I am sure of it," he said as he tied her ankles. "Perhaps another time and another place will come."

A touch of sadness pulled at her handsome face. "It won't. I know that. You know that," she said.

"I never say never," he returned. "I'll be near. Call if you need me." She nodded and lay back, and Fargo stretched out a few yards from her. He stayed awake as the night came, thoughts still whirling through his mind. When the moon began to travel across the sky, he rose and went to where Jessica slept. He put one hand over her mouth and she woke at once, eyes wide. "It's me. Don't make noise," he said and took his hand away.

"What is it?" she asked, sitting up.

"Get dressed. Quietly. You're going riding," he said and stepped back. This time she didn't go behind a tree to change but let the sheet drop, a taunting gesture he wished he had time to respond to. When she was dressed he led her to a small mound at the edge of the trees and pointed to a draw bathed in moonlight. "You go through there, riding hard as you can. At the end of it you'll see a long stand of red cedar. Stay in the cedar and keep heading east. When the cedar ends there'll be a forest of bur oak. A rough road runs alongside it. Take the road until it becomes a low plain. Ride the plain east and you'll come to the stockade. You've been there. You'll recognize the land around it."

"Through the draw, the red cedar, alongside the bur oak, and onto the low plain. I have it. What happens when I reach the stockade?" she questioned.

"Tell the general to take every damn trooper he can spare and ride to the forest of box elder northwest of the stockade. He'll know where that is. Tell him to go through the center of the box elder till he finds a wide, fast-running stream. He follows the stream west and he'll come to Red Hawk's camp. He attacks as fast and as hard as he can."

"Where will you be?" Jessica asked.

"Trying to keep Red Hawk from slaughtering the hostages," Fargo said. "It'll be tomorrow night before you reach the stockade. Tell the general I want him on his way come dawn at a full gallop."

"What if I get lost and get there late? What if he gets to Red Hawk's camp late?" Jessica asked as he walked back to the gelding with her.

"Nothing good," he said. She paused and suddenly her mouth was on his, pressed hard.

"Till next time," she said as she pulled away and swung onto the gelding. She walked the horse and he heard her go into a canter only after he'd lost sight of her in the dark. He returned to where Moonrise slept, stretched out, and found sleep for himself until morning came. He rose, then untied her, and she stretched, her eyes traveling across the scene.

"Where is Jess-ee-ka?" she asked at once.

"Gone," he said.

"You sent her away?" Moonrise questioned, black eyes narrowing.

"I don't know what will happen. Somebody should come

142

out of this alive," he said, and she thought about his answer.

"Let me go back alone. Follow her. Save yourself, too," Moonrise said.

"I made an agreement. I'll keep my part," Fargo said.

Her shrug was a resigned gesture. "Then we go now," she said.

"No. We stay," he said, and her eyes widened.

"Why?"

He did not want her growing suspicious, did not want to give her an added reason to run. "When your warriors go into battle, they first dance the war dances, sing the war chants, pray to the Great Spirit. They prepare themselves for what they must do. I must prepare myself," he said.

She frowned back. "It is not the way of your people," she said.

"It is, in our own ways," he answered, and she thought for a moment. He saw her decide to accept his answer.

"I am sorry. It will not change anything," she said with a trace of sullenness.

It was his turn to shrug. "We'll see," he said and stretched out beside her. She had shared the terrible truth of Red Hawk's plans with him. She would have enjoyed sharing her body with him. Those things had been made clear. The loyalty of gratitude and the power of physical attraction had been very real. But now it had all changed, subtly yet with equal reality. She was nearing home. The loyalty of heritage and the power of ancestry were in control now. Blood was thicker than water. Her loyalties had shifted, perhaps reluctantly, yet very definitely. But she had been willing to accept his answer about preparing. She understood that. It was also part of her heritage. He lay motionless on the ground with his eyes open, staring ahead in what seemed total concentration.

In a way he was doing exactly that, his thoughts concentrating on what had to be done, counting off hours, minutes, seconds. Timing was essential, yet for the most part beyond his control. Jessica had to reach the stockade in time, and Miles Stanford had to attack at the right moment. If he were too early, he'd face Red Hawk and all his warriors, resulting in a giant bloodbath for everyone. Red Hawk would certainly order the hostages slain in the battle. If he arrived too late, the hostages would already have been slain. Timing was the key to all of it. The only part he had any chance of controlling was outfoxing Red Hawk—and even that was far from a certainty.

Yet his plan was the only one that might possibly work. He had to trick the Kiowa into dividing his forces in two. That would let the troops easily overcome the first half, with the Kiowa too hard-pressed to bother with the hostages. Then they'd do the same when the second half returned. It was the only chance, he repeated to himself, and cursed inwardly. The spin of a roulette wheel held better odds. He forced himself to relax and glanced at Moonrise. She lay with the stoicism that was part of her. He rose when the sun began to slide toward the horizon. She was on her feet at once. "We ride," he said, and she swung onto the Ovaro in front of him.

"You have taken a lot of time," she said accusingly. "We will not make my father's camp today."

"That's right. Tomorrow morning," he said and sent the Ovaro eastward. She rode in silence with him, and when night fell he halted at a glen of wild plum. They finished the dried beef strips he had and ate the wild plums as a treat to end the meal. When he was finished, he tied Moonrise again and slept beside her. Rising first with the morning sun, he was dressed and quickly untied her after she woke. He swept the land with a long glance as time ticked away in his mind. They were almost too close for what he wanted. He spotted the glistening blue of a small pond. "There is no hurry. You can wash in that pond," he said.

"No. Just take me back," she said. "There will be many other ponds later."

He swore silently and stepped closer to her. "Then you will stay here until I come back," he said, and Moonrise searched his face as she frowned.

"Where are you going?" she questioned.

"Things I must do," he said, wrapping the lariat around her waist and leading her to one of the trees. She continued to frown at him as he tied her to the tree, waist and ankles first, then bound her wrists together. "You go to my father's camp," she said, and his silence was an admission. "You lied about preparing yourself for battle. You did not prepare. You planned," she accused.

"Same thing," he returned.

"No. One is of the spirit, the other of trickery," she said.

"It is your father who knows about trickery," Fargo said.

Her eyes flashed. "He knows about being tricked," she said defensively.

"You have more honor," he told her. "You spoke the truth to me."

"Let me go to him. Let me change his mind," she said.

"You know that won't happen," Fargo said. "Don't turn from truth to lies." He paused, let his eyes scan the terrain once more. She said nothing, but her eyes bored into him, anger and pain in their dark depths. He turned from her, climbed onto the Ovaro, and paused. "You have nothing to fear. I will come back for you—or he will," Fargo said.

"There is only fear left for me. Fear for you who saved me and fear for my father who sent you," she answered. "Leave me." He had no reply for the bitterness and truth in her words. He put the Ovaro into a fast canter. He didn't look back as he rode through the lush greenery that would have been welcome under other circumstances. He rode hard, one eye on the sun as it began to rise higher over the treetops. He slowed the pinto to a trot and finally into a walk as he saw the long stand of box elder. The sound of the fast-running stream came to him, and then the Kiowa camp came into sight through the trees.

He kept the horse at a walk as he entered the camp, moving down the very center of it as the squaws and naked children parted for him. The braves stood their ground and watched him with hostile eyes as he reined to a halt in front of the largest tipi. Red Hawk stepped out of the wigwam, the long necklace of hawks' talons brushing his powerful chest. His face sternly impassive, his eyes burned with piercing brightness as he waited with icy imperiousness. Charlie Sycamore was no longer on hand to translate, and Fargo wondered how the chief intended to communicate with him. That question was answered as the Kiowa chief gestured and a small, elderly figure in nothing but a breechclout shuffled forward. "I will speak for Red Hawk," the man said. Fargo guessed he had once sold to trading posts.

"I have brought back Moonrise," Fargo said.

The small man translated, and Fargo saw Red Hawk's face offer not the slightest change in expression. "I do not see her," the Kiowa said.

"I will bring her after you let the prisoners go," Fargo said.

"You bring her first," Red Hawk said through his translator.

"Let me see the hostages," Fargo answered.

"They are alive. They wait," the Indian returned.

"Let me see," Fargo said, stubbornness coming into his voice.

Red Hawk motioned for him to follow as he started through the trees. A dozen braves and the small elderly man also followed as Fargo stayed atop the Ovaro. The curtain of trees thinned, and Fargo saw the wagons with some ten braves standing guard around them. The settlers in and near their wagons started forward at once as they saw Fargo, but the Kiowa guards stepped in quickly and pushed them back. "You have seen. Now bring Moonrise," Red Hawk said.

Fargo's gaze swept the hostages, saw the flare of hope in every pair of eyes, and cursed inwardly. They tasted freedom, their lives being given back to them. But he knew the reality. They were closer to death than ever before. His eyes flicked skyward for a moment. The sun continued to rise higher in a yellow sky. If the general was charging his way, the next minutes would mean survival or death. Fargo returned his eyes to the Kiowa chief. "Let them go," he said.

"Moonrise," Red Hawk said. "Bring Moonrise first."

Fargo set his jaw. "No. I keep her till you let them go," he said.

Red Hawk's stern face slid into almost a sneer as he barked at his braves. "Keep him here," he ordered with a gesture to Fargo, and six of the Indians instantly surrounded the horse, tugging at the rider. Fargo swung to the ground.

"This won't bring you Moonrise," Fargo said to the chief.

"I bring her back myself," Red Hawk said and almost laughed.

"You won't find her," Fargo said, but let sudden alarm color his voice.

Red Hawk cast a glance of contempt at him. "You have her near, close enough so you can bring her to me. My braves will search. They will find her. You make mistake. It is over for you," he said with the help of his translator.

Fargo let himself look thoroughly alarmed. "No, you can't find her," he said.

Red Hawk uttered a contemptuous sound. One of the braves ran into the trees, returning in moments with some thirty others. With the others standing by, they made up about half of Red Hawk's force, Fargo calculated. A brave brought a pinto pony for Red Hawk, and the chief pulled himself onto the horse. He cast a victoriously smug glance at Fargo. "We will find her. You know this. It is over for you and the others," he said.

Fargo protested as he let fear color his face now. "This is not right. I have brought her all this way," he said. But he let helpless chagrin flood his face now, and the Kiowa tossed back a curse as he rode off with his braves. Ten braves remained, guarding those in the wagons, and now him, Fargo saw. But it had gone exactly as he had planned, and he flashed another glance at the sky. The sun continued to move across the morning sky, and Fargo forced himself to relax. The Colt lay in its holster, but each of the Kiowa held rifles, some Hawkens frontier rifles, some army carbines, all captured trophies. It was not time for desperation tactics yet.

Red Hawk and the others had faded from hearing. They would spread out in a straight line and comb the terrain. They would find her, he knew. He could only wait and desperately hope Miles Stanford arrived before Red Hawk found his daughter. He squatted on the ground, stretched, rose, moved toward the wagons, and two of the braves stepped forward at once. Fargo shrugged and retreated to the Ovaro, cast another glance skyward, and knew the perspiration that coated his chest did not come from the sun's rays alone. Time seemed to hang in a void, not moving at all, while at the same time moving with furious speed. He found himself pacing back and forth, the length of the Ovaro, when he suddenly stopped, frozen in position.

The sound came to his ears first, and then he saw the Kiowa guards pick it up, and suddenly it was more than sound as the ground vibrated with the thunder of hooves. He heard the bugle split the air as, beyond the curtain of trees, the general's troops charged into the Kiowa camp. Gunfire resounded, the staccato bark of the troopers' carbines. The Kiowa camp had been taken by surprise, he knew, and he crouched as the ten Kiowa guards raced through the trees to go to the support of the others. Fargo stayed in a crouch as the ten guards disappeared into the trees, then swung onto the Ovaro and paused as he saw those in the wagons begin to gather children to flee.

"No," he said. "Stay here. You'll only get yourselves killed in the cross fire if you try to run." They stopped, fell back, and Fargo sent the Ovaro racing through the trees. He charged into the rear of the Kiowa camp to see the ground littered with near-naked bodies, individual combat still going on at the sides and at the stream. But most of the troopers were regrouping, and he saw the general come toward him. "Right on time, thank God," Fargo said.

"Get some new gray hairs?" Miles asked.

"Too many," Fargo said as the last of the gunfire died away.

"Jessica did a fine job of reaching us," the general said. "Where are the hostages she spoke about?"

"This way," Fargo said and led the general and most of his troops through the trees to the back clearing, where the hostages ran forward to embrace the troopers. "It's not over," Fargo said to Miles. "Red Hawk will be coming back with the other half of his men. He may be on his way now."

Miles pulled his lips back in distaste. "I've got at least

ten wounded. I'll be hard-pressed fighting that many Kiowa again. Let me get my men into the trees and set up an ambush. That'll give us an edge. I'll clear the hostages away, too."

"No," Fargo said and drew a frown from the general. "Red Hawk will know something's gone wrong if they're not in place," Fargo said.

"Hell, Fargo, we can't ask them to stay in the middle of a pitched battle, not after all they've been through," Miles said.

"No, but we can ask them to change clothes," Fargo answered, and the general's eyes took but a split second to light up.

"Jesus, yes, that's it," he said and immediately turned to where the troopers and hostages had gathered together. He spoke quickly to the hostages, in terse yet concerned words, and Fargo turned the Ovaro back into the heavy tree cover. He dismounted and knelt down on one knee to wait. The kind of hatred Red Hawk carried gave him an added canniness, a heightened awareness that was characteristic of every predator. It would be the last wait, Fargo knew, and there was no assurance it would go well.

9

The small area of thinned trees was silent, the wagons in place, men lounging near the empty wagon shafts, women, most in their bonnets, visible through the tailgate openings. Perhaps an hour had passed since the general's first attack on the Kiowa camp, and Fargo's eyes swept the trees where he waited. Some fifteen troopers were poised, carbines at the ready. He spied the general at the far end, crouched and waiting, his heavy army Colt in hand. Fargo brought his eyes back to the distant row of box elder and saw the sudden movement of branches. He waited a moment more, saw the branches move again in a steady line coming toward them.

He rose and saw the general turn to him at once. A whispered command and the troopers dropped to one knee, carbines raised to fire. Fargo's eyes were riveted on the line of branches, which continued to quiver. It was but minutes when he saw the Kiowa appear through the trees. Red Hawk was in the first knot of riders, and Fargo thought he caught a glimpse of Moonrise farther back, surrounded by other braves. That made sense. Red Hawk was too cautious to have her up in front. The Kiowa chief reached the edge of the trees and cast a glance at the wagons and the figures inside them. He started to go on, then suddenly snapped his eyes back to the wagons. With a shout, Red Hawk whirled and barked commands, and Fargo saw the others also spin as they dived from their horses.

But he heard Miles shout the command to fire, and the trees where he waited erupted in a fusillade. However, the Kiowa were into their tree cover and firing back. "God-damn," Fargo bit out as he suddenly realized what Red Hawk had seen, and he cursed the man's canniness. The surprise of ambush hadn't been destroyed, but it had certainly been diminished, and the Kiowa, firing from cover now, returned rifle and arrow fire. Fargo, moving in a crouch, began to circle through the trees at his end of the box elder. When he reached where the Kiowa fired back, he dropped to his stomach and began to crawl.

Miles would be sending troops from the other side to outflank the Kiowa, he knew. That'd be standard military tactics. And they had gotten off the first volley. They had done the initial damage. Red Hawk was too smart a warrior not to know that his forces were in trouble. He was also smart enough to know when it was time to retreat and save his skin. Fargo lifted his head to peer through the foliage. He was behind some of the Kiowa, across from others. He spotted close to a dozen bodies on the ground. As he watched, a brave half rose to fire an arrow—and went down as a bullet smashed into him.

Fargo's eyes continued to search the battle scene. At the far end, he spotted the powerfully built figure with the talon necklace. Red Hawk was firing an army carbine and edging his way to the rear of the trees, where a dozen Indian ponies were visible. Fargo rose, exchanged speed for stealth, and began to race through the trees, the Colt in hand. A Kiowa saw him rise and started to bring his rifle around. But Fargo's shot caught him full in the chest and he sailed backward. Another two Kiowa spied him and half rose to fire. Fargo fired again, and the nearest Indian went down as his head exploded. The second one half spun and gasped out in pain as a trooper's bullet tore into his back. Fargo kept running, dropping to a half crouch, and saw Red Hawk catch sight of him. The Kiowa chief turned, carbine in hand, and ran for the ponies. Fargo veered sharply to cut the distance, fired, and missed as Red Hawk ran behind a tree trunk and continued in tall brush beyond the tree.

Fargo flung himself sideways as an arrow grazed his head, hit the ground rolling, executed a somersault, and came up firing at the figure charging toward him with up-raised tomahawk. The brave quivered as his midsection turned red, and he collapsed face forward on the ground. Fargo had already turned and raced toward the ponies, his eyes searching for Red Hawk. He had almost reached the ponies, but the Kiowa chief was nowhere in sight. Fargo skidded to a halt, alarm spiraling through him. He started to drop to the ground when the figure hurtled down onto him from a tree. He tried to bring one hand up but a rifle butt slammed into the side of his temple and he went down, the world exploding in a shower of red, yellow, and purple stars.

He managed to bring the Colt up, firing as he did, wild shots, but they made Red Hawk duck away. Fargo used the moment to roll, shake his head, and the world returned. He saw the Indian charging at him, and he brought the Colt up again, fired, and heard the click of the hammer on an empty chamber. He threw the pistol at Red Hawk's charging figure, caught the man alongside the cheek, and the Kiowa chief stumbled before he caught himself. Fargo dived forward, low, wrapped his arms around the Indian's legs, and both men went down. Fargo drove his forearm into the Indian's throat and Red Hawk gasped for wind as Fargo tore the carbine from his grip. Rolling away from his opponent, Fargo brought the carbine up and fired—and again heard the sound of an empty gun. He cursed as he raised the rifle by the barrel and swung it, using the stock as a club. But Red Hawk dropped down and the rifle passed over his head. The Kiowa bulled forward, sank a powerful blow into Fargo's abdomen, and the Trailsman fell back—it was his moment to gasp for breath.

Red Hawk charged again, powerful arms outstretched, closing around Fargo's neck. His weight carried Fargo back and down. Fargo saw the Indian reach one hand out and bring it up, clutching a rock. He brought the rock down and Fargo had just enough time to twist his head away so the blow grazed his head. Bringing one knee up, Fargo drove it into Red Hawk's ribs, and the Indian grunted as he fell sideways. It was enough for Fargo to kick out, land a foot in his foe's belly, and twist away. But the Kiowa chief rolled, came up on his feet, and charged again. This time he had grabbed the carbine. He rushed, using it as a spear.

Fargo sidestepped at the last moment as the barrel of the gun was about to rip into his abdomen, driving his shoulder into Red Hawk as the man went by. The Indian stumbled to the side, turned with the rifle in hand, but Fargo's swinging left landed on the point of his jaw. It was a blow that would have finished most men, but the Kiowa's powerful figure staggered, took two steps backward, and started forward again with the rifle. Fargo backed, crouched, his hand yanking at the calf holster around his leg. Red Hawk charged as Fargo brought the thin-bladed knife up. The Kiowa glimpsed the weapon, twisted to shift his charge, and Fargo stuck one leg out as Red Hawk thundered by. The Kiowa fell and Fargo was atop him at once, before the Indian had a chance to do more than half turn. Fargo's hand held the blade against

Red Hawk's throat as he straddled the man. The Kiowa chief froze, slowly opened his hand, and let the carbine fall to the ground.

Dimly, Fargo heard the sound of rifle fire still popping in the distance, but there was nothing dim in the voice that came to him. "Let him go," it said with deadly clearness. Fargo kept the knife blade against the Kiowa chief's throat but stayed motionless. He didn't need to turn his head; Moonrise's voice was completely familiar to him.

"Stay out of this," Fargo said, not moving, the knife pressed against the man's throat.

"Let him go," Moonrise said again.

Fargo stayed unmoving. "Kill me and I'll still cut his throat before I die," he said.

"Let him go or I kill her," Moonrise said. Fargo felt the surprise sweep through him, and this time he did turn his head as he kept the knife in place. He stared at Jessica as she stood quietly, Moonrise holding a revolver to her temple.

"What in hell are you doing here?" Fargo growled.

"Good God, this is no time for pointless questions," Jessica said. He grimaced at the truth of the reply and brought his eyes to Moonrise.

"What happens if I let him go?" he asked.

"We run. You have won. The bluecoats have won," Moonrise said.

Fargo studied the black eyes that burned with more whirling emotions than he could sort out. But there was one he didn't need to question, echoed in the absolute steadiness of her hand holding the revolver. She read the thoughts as they raced through his mind. "He is my father," she said.

"Tell him one wrong move and I'll kill him," Fargo said.

She barked words at Red Hawk, and Fargo saw the man nod his head. Fargo pushed up from where he straddled the

Kiowa chief and drew the knife back. The Indian rose, shot a look of hatred at him, and started toward Moonrise. Fargo saw her step away from Jessica and come forward with two ponies. Red Hawk pulled himself on one and Moonrise swung onto the other. The chief paused as he wheeled his pony to look back.

"It will never be over," he said. "There will be another time." Moonrise translated the pledge for Fargo.

Fargo's eyes went to her. "You have anything to leave me with?" he asked. She waited a moment, her eyes on him, and then she opened the top of the elkhide dress and let it fall to her waist. The high, round, smooth breasts swayed together as she let him once more see the primitive copper-hued beauty of her. With a sudden wild yet musical laugh, she raced away with her father to disappear into the forest.

"What was that all about?" Jessica asked.

"About reminding, about having the last word, about winning in the way a woman can always win," Fargo said.

"I've got better ways," Jessica said, and he came along beside her as they walked through the trees.

"Now, I'll ask it again—what in hell are you doing here? Miles wouldn't have brought you along," Fargo said.

"He didn't. I followed. I heard the fighting. When it seemed to die down I circled closer."

"And Moonrise saw you," Fargo said, and she nodded a little sheepishly.

"You ever really obey anything?" he grumbled.

"You're not the only one who has to see things through," she said. "None of this would've worked if it hadn't been for me."

"True enough," he conceded.

"And you still have a lot to make up for," she said.

"And I know just how I'm going to do it," he said.

"You're damn right," Jessica said. "Starting tonight." She pressed her breast against him for emphasis. Not that he needed any. This was one kind of command he'd enjoy obeying.

LOOKING FORWARD!
The following is the opening
section from the next novel in the exciting
Trailsman series from Signet:

**THE TRAILSMAN #169
SOCORRO SLAUGHTER**

*1860, New Mexico Territory—
where hatred had spawned a killing ground . . .*

When a man has ridden a horse day after day, month after month, he gets to know that animal as well as he knows himself.

Skye Fargo was no exception. Like many a horseman, he thought of his Ovaro more as a companion than a simple beast of burden. He knew its moods, knew the limits to which he could push the pinto stallion without running it into the ground. He knew how it would react in any given situation. He also knew the many sounds it made and what each sound meant.

So when the horse gave out with a low, rumbling nicker in the middle of the night, Skye Fargo was instantly awake, his hand on the Colt strapped to his right hip. He gave a single shake of his head to clear lingering cobwebs, then strained his senses to learn why the Ovaro was agitated.

The answer became clear moments later when the crisp

breeze carried a faint crunch to Fargo's ears, just such a noise as a foot stepping on gravel might make.

Fargo rolled onto his left side and pushed into a crouch, facing southwest, the direction the sound came from. Earlier that night he'd made camp in chaparral which bordered the narrow dusty road from Albuquerque to Las Cruces, a normal precaution in a territory plagued by Apache and Navaho marauders. He'd figured that he was so well hidden, no one could find him.

Evidently he had been mistaken.

Fargo removed his hat and leaned it against his saddle, which he had been using as a pillow. Then, after hiking his blanket high enough to give the impression there was someone under it, he crept into the dark and hunkered behind a cluster of mesquite.

The telltale jingle of spurs told Fargo his visitors weren't Indians, since no self-respecting warrior would be caught dead in them. His lake-blue eyes narrowed when he saw a shadow detach itself from a bush several dozen yards away and move toward the stallion. There was something about the shadow which bothered him. It was on all fours, low to the ground as a slinking man would be, but it moved too quickly, too smoothly to be human.

Then it hit him. The creature was a dog, not a man. Now Fargo understood how his camp had been discovered; the dog had picked up the Ovaro's scent.

Fargo held himself as still as the mesquite, his thumb on the hammer of the pistol. Behind the dog other shapes had appeared, three of them moving quietly forward, their features shrouded by *sombreros*. Moonlight glittered dully off six-shooters.

Bandidos, Fargo reasoned. Back in Albuquerque he'd

heard tell that a band of bandits was making life miserable for folks living in the vicinity of Socorro. These men might be part of that band.

The dog proved to be well trained. It advanced to within a few yards of the small clearing and paused to sniff. The stallion watched closely with head held high and ears pricked, but the dog paid it no attention. All the dog seemed interested in was the blanket.

Fargo saw one of the figures glide up close to the mongrel. At a whispered word, the dog stalked toward the saddle. Body bent lower than ever, lips pulled back to reveal tapered teeth, it moved a few feet, froze for several seconds, then moved a little farther.

The stallion stamped a front hoof, causing the dog to swivel around. It appeared about to attack but a sharp gesture by the figure sent it on its way again.

Slowly raising the Colt, Fargo took deliberate aim at the dog's head. The animal was more dangerous than the bandits and had to be taken care of first. He started to ease back the hammer slowly so the click would not be all that loud.

To Fargo's chagrin, the dog heard. It immediately whirled toward the mesquite and growled. Fargo shifted the pistol slightly to compensate and squeezed the trigger, but just as he did the beast lunged to the left and streaked into the chaparral.

At the retort, all hell broke loose. The Ovaro reared and whinnied shrilly while the three bandits cut loose, their revolvers spitting flame and smoke, the night rocking to the thunder of gun blasts.

Lead clipped limbs and smacked into the ground on both sides of Fargo as he threw himself to the left and rolled.

Through a gap he spied one of the trio. Banging off a pair of swift shots, he rose onto his right knee and was about to rush deeper into the mesquite to outflank the cutthroats when a lightning form hurtled out of nowhere and caught him flush on the shoulder.

The impact bowled Fargo over. He nearly cried out when razor teeth sheared through his buckskin shirt into his flesh, drawing a spurt of blood. Flat on his back, he lashed out, clubbing the dog across the skull as it let go of his shoulder and snapped at his neck. The blow staggered the animal long enough for Fargo to scramble backward, out of reach of those deadly fangs.

Or so he thought.

Fargo snapped the Colt high to put a slug into the mongrel, yet as fast as he was, the dog was faster. It pounced, those iron jaws clamping shut on his wrist. Waves of pain coursed up his arm. His instinctive reaction was to jerk his arm loose but he knew that in doing so he would shred his own wrist so he kicked the dog instead. His boot heel slammed into the brute's front legs so hard they were knocked out from under it.

The beast let go. Fargo pivoted and trained the barrel on its temple. He would have fired had not one of the bandits hurtled out of the brush. A six-gun roared and Fargo answered in kind. The *bandido* stumbled, cursed in Spanish, then fell.

Fargo again went to slay the dog but it had more lives than a cat and was on him before he could squeeze the trigger. This time it came straight for his jugular, snarling and bristling in bestial rage. Without thinking, he shoved his gun arm under the animal's lower jaw and held it briefly at bay while scrabbling to the left.

The dog went into a frenzy. It bit and tore at Fargo, tearing his sleeve wide open and ripping into his skin. He battered it with his other arm and continued to kick, but the rain of blows had no effect.

Keenly aware that the third bandit might show up at any moment, Fargo coiled both legs and drove them into the mongrel's belly. The dog went flying, recovered in a heartbeat, and, undaunted, sprang once more.

This time Fargo was ready. He fanned the Colt, three shots so closely spaced they sounded like one. It was as if an invisible hammer smashed into the dog, catapulting it head over heels into the nearest bush.

Fargo gained his feet and crouched, waiting for the last bandit to appear. He quickly reloaded.

The dog twitched and growled and tried to stand but couldn't. Defiant to the last, it snarled at him before sinking limply to the arid soil.

A minute went by, then several more. All Fargo heard was the wind rustling the mesquite and the nervous prancing of the stallion. He straightened when a distant drumming of hoofs revealed the last *bandido* had had enough and was headed for parts unknown. Lowering the Colt, he breathed in deeply to calm his racing pulse.

Before Fargo could take stock of his wounds, he had to check the others. The dog didn't move when he nudged it. Pressing his hand to its neck, he confirmed the beast was dead. The same held true for the second bandit.

Veering to the clearing, Fargo found the first *bandido* lying face down in a spreading inky pool. Fargo kicked the man's pistol out of reach, then knelt and placed his hand on the killer's shoulder.

Groaning loudly, the bandit opened his eyes. He was

swarthy, his chin covered with stubble, his mustache slick with grease. Blood trickled from the corners of his mouth when he tried to speak and a fit of coughing racked him. Finally, he sputtered *"Diablo?"*

Making a guess, Fargo answered, "The dog is dead."

The *bandido* sighed. "That is too bad, gringo. *Diablo* was a good *perro*. He served me well." The man bit his lower lip for a short while. "Before I go, I would like to know who you are."

Fargo offered no reply.

"Is it so much for a man to ask?" the bandit said weakly. "What is wrong with wanting to know the name of the *hombre* who has done what so many others were not able to do? Because of you, I will soon be burning in the eternal fire. The least you can do is tell me."

Wary of a trick, Fargo bent down and did as the killer wanted.

"Gracias. I am Pedro Valdez. Let others know, *por favor.* I want word to get back to my parents in Chihuahua. They are the only ones who will give a damn." More coughing caused the bandit to quake and moan.

Fargo checked for hidden weapons and discovered a dagger in Valdez's boot and a derringer wedged under the cutthroat's wide brown leather belt. "Were you waiting for me to turn my back?"

Valdez mustered a wan grin. "A man can always hope, senor." He inhaled raggedly. "You are a tough one. I can see that. But there is one who is tougher. Stay in this country a while and Santiago will pay you back for what you have done this night. Yes, *hombre.* Santiago will—"

The words trailed off. Pedro Valdez uttered a long sigh which ended in a strangled gasp.

Fargo stepped to the saddle and shrugged out of his shirt. The dog had done slight damage to his wrist but his shoulder was another matter. A two-inch gash, half as deep, still bled freely. He had to cauterize it before the loss of blood weakened him.

Using the pile of kindling he had gathered before turning in, Fargo soon had his small campfire rekindled. From his right boot he took the Arkansas toothpick he favored and heated the slender blade in the dancing flames. Soon the knife was hot enough. He stuffed part of his shirt into his mouth, clamped down, and then applied the blade to the gash.

There was loud sizzling. Searing agony lanced through the Trailsman. The acrid scent of burnt flesh filled his nostrils, and for a couple of seconds the stars spun crazily. He bowed his head until the sickening sensation passed.

Running his fingers over the wound, Fargo confirmed that the knife had done its job. The bleeding had indeed stopped. Now he only had to worry about infection setting in.

After sliding the toothpick into its ankle sheath, Fargo dressed, sat on the blanket, and awaited the dawn. Sleep was out of the question. As a precaution, he took his heavy-caliber Sharps from the saddle scabbard and rested the rifle across his legs.

In ten days Fargo had to be in Las Cruces. Much closer, only a few hours to the south, was Socorro. He would have plenty of time to stop there for a spell and let his wound mend some before he pushed on.

Traveling in a weakened state in the Territory of New Mexico wasn't advisable. The land was as hard as flint, as merciless as a Mescalero on the war path. The most simple of mistakes could well prove deadly, which was why scores of pilgrims lost their lives every year. A single moment's carelessness was all it took.

Fargo had learned the hard way not to take the land or its people for granted. When on the go, he made it a habit to check his back trail frequently. When camping, he picked out of the way places and kept his fires small, as would an Indian. When in the desert, he knew how to find water where most whites had no idea it would be. In the mountains he could find game without half trying.

So although Fargo had been wounded, he wasn't worried. He didn't do as many greenhorns would have done, and panicked. Keeping his wits was another important trait experience had taught him.

The man who lost his head was more apt to lose his life.

Sunrise was an hour off when Fargo made a pot of coffee and downed two cups of the piping hot brew. As pink-and-yellow bands streaked the eastern horizon, he rose and went in search of the mounts belonging to the slain bandits. He half hoped the animals had run off so he wouldn't need to tote the corpses into Socorro, but as luck would have it he located a bay and a sorrel hidden in the chaparral about two hundred yards from the clearing. Neither shied when he grabbed their reins and led them back.

A golden crown framed the skyline when Fargo stepped into the stirrups and wound his way through the chaparral to the road. Pointing the stallion due south, he rode at a trot for the first mile to put some distance between himself and the clearing in case the *bandido* who got away returned with friends.

Presently four riders appeared, heading north. They were cowhands, though, and they gave Fargo a wide berth when they spotted the bodies. So did the driver of a buckboard, half an hour later. The man cracked his whip to spur the team on while the elderly woman beside him covered the lowered portion of her face with a red shawl and gawked at the bodies through eyes the size of walnuts.

It wasn't long afterward that Socorro came into sight, its many long, low buildings close to the Rio Grande, which glistened to the east.

Fargo looked neither right nor left as he entered the town and rode down the middle of the main street. Still, there was no mistaking the sensation he created. Many passersby halted to study the bodies. Men fingered rifles or pistols. Women grasped small children and made them look away. Several dogs added to the commotion by darting out of a side street and yipping like loco coyotes.

In front of a saloon Fargo drew rein. He looped the reins to all three horses around the hitch rail, swiped dust from his buckskins, and sauntered into the cool, gloomy interior.

"What's your poison, stranger?" the beanpole barkeep asked.

"A bottle of the best tonsil varnish you've got," Fargo declared, striding to the bar and slapping enough coins to cover the cost onto the counter.

The bartender eyed Fargo's torn shoulder and sleeve, his brow knit. "Looks to me as if you've earned the treat. Had a lick of trouble, did you?"

"Does the name Pedro Valdez mean anything to you?"

It was an innocent question on Fargo's part. He started to reach for the bottle but the barkeep went rigid in the act of handing it over. So did everyone else in the saloon, and the place became as silent as a tomb. Fargo scanned the room, then chuckled. "From the look of things, Valdez must be one popular fella."

"Are you joshing, mister?" the bartender said. "Valdez is the second most wanted man in all of New Mexico. He's a born killer from south of the border who joined up with the Maxwell gang a while back. There's no telling how many innocent people he's butchered. Why, if he was to walk in here right this minute, I'd throttle him with my bare hands."

Fargo got hold of the bottle and opened it. "Be my guest, friend."

"How's that?"

"Valdez is right outside. You're welcome to go out and strangle the daylights out of him if you want." Fargo tipped the whiskey and drank greedily, feeling the liquid scorch a path down his throat, washing away the dust of the trail. He ignored the mass exodus as the customers flocked to the batwing doors. By the time they straggled back inside he had a third of the bottle polished off and a warm glow in the pit of his stomach.

In the lead was the bartender. "I don't believe it, stranger! You made wolf meat of Pedro Valdez!"

Fargo set down the bottle and smacked his lips. "It's a habit of mine when someone is trying to kill me."

"I'm Joe O'Keefe," the man said while moving behind the bar. "A cousin of mine was cut to ribbons by the Maxwell gang four months ago, along with the pretty filly he was fixing to marry." His voice choked with emotion. "I was real fond of young Ed. He was going to go to law school back East to make something of himself." O'Keefe pushed the coins toward Fargo. "So you can keep your money. That bottle is on the house, and anything else you want, to boot."

Suddenly Fargo was surrounded by beaming citizens of Socorro who clapped him on the back and thanked him over and over. Their gratitude was genuine but it made Fargo feel uncomfortable. Killing Valdez had been a sheer fluke, the result of being in the wrong place at the wrong time. He didn't feel right being made out to be some kind of hero.

"It's too bad the marshal is off delivering a prisoner up to Santa Fe," O'Keefe remarked. "Otherwise he'd be in here buying you all the drinks you could down. He's been after Valdez for months now but never saw hide nor hair of the vermin."

"Who can blame him?" a patron said. "Maxwell was raised in this part of the country and knows it better than anyone. There ain't a man alive who can track him to his lair."

O'Keefe, partly in jest, addressed Fargo. "Maybe you'd like to try, mister. Put windows in that buzzard's skull and you'll be the toast of the whole territory. Hell, we'd vote you in as governor in a landslide."

"I'm just passing through."

From the front of the saloon a deep voice boomed. "That's a crying shame, mister. Maybe five thousand dollars will get you to change your mind."

Another hush fell over the room as all eyes swiveled toward the speaker, a beefy man who packed more corded muscle on his stout frame than most five men combined. It showed in the rippling layers on his neck and huge hands as he bulled his way through the ring of admirers to confront Fargo. His face was seamed with wrinkles and had been bronzed by long exposure to the sun. His clothes and wide brimmed hat marked him as a man of means, a rancher, perhaps, judging by the large callouses Fargo felt when they shook hands.

"William Ragsdale is my handle, and I own the Bar R, just about the biggest spread this side of the Rio Grande. Who might you be?"

"Skye Fargo."

Ragsdale blinked and stepped back to give Fargo a closer scrutiny. "That name is familiar for some reason. Do I know you from somewhere?"

"It's a small world."

Crooking an elbow, the rancher leaned on the counter. "I reckon. So what do you say to the five thousand?"

The notion of earning so much money was tantalizing. Fargo was like most men and enjoyed living high on the hog on occasion. Games of high stakes poker, nights spent in the company of willing doves, and eating at classy restaurants were some of his favorite pastimes, but they did not come cheap. He was tempted until he thought of his appointment in Las Cruces. It was bound to take longer than a week and a half to track Maxwell down.

William Ragsdale took the pause as an encouraging sign. "Ask any man here. I'm as good as my word. If you kill Maxwell, I'll have the cash in your hand before the body is cold."

"If you want him planted so badly, why not round up a bunch of your hands and do it yourself?"

Someone coughed nervously but the rancher didn't take offense. "Do you think I haven't tried? Fifteen, twenty times, at least. He's struck my ranch more often than I care to count, bushwhacking my punchers or slaughtering cattle for the sheer hell of it. Each time he got away as slick as could be."

Excerpt from SOCORRO SLAUGHTER

"He's bound to slip up sooner or later," Fargo said, and swallowed more rotgut.

The rancher snorted. "I can see that you don't know what we're dealing with here. Santiago Maxwell is a half-breed. His pa was a breed himself, part Mexican, part Navaho. His ma was white trash. Think about that mix a minute. To make things worse, he lived with the tribe for a few years when he was younger, and he learned all their heathen ways. There isn't a white man alive who can match him in the wild." Ragsdale paused. "But something tells me you could."

"I have business elsewhere," Fargo explained. He would have gone on but for a most aromatic fragrance which seemed to fill the room all at once. Turning, he beheld the source, a redheaded vision of loveliness in a tight riding outfit who was striding boldly toward them.

"Pa, I'm tired of waiting out in that awful sun. How much longer are you going to be?"

The customers parted to let her through, every man there doffing his hat in respect, a few averting their eyes as if afraid to gaze at her.

The vision was heedless of them all. She was in her early twenties with a complexion as smooth as glass and an hourglass figure most women would die for. Her eyes were sparkling blue, her lips the color of ripe cherries.

"Virginia!" Ragsdale barked. "A proper lady doesn't enter saloons! Go outside and wait until I'm done. I'm trying to persuade this gentleman to go after Maxwell for us."

Grinning impishly, the daughter regarded Fargo a few moments, then draped her slim hands on her shapely hips. "I do so hope you will agree, mister. We haven't had a prime specimen like you in these parts in ages."

Ragsdale flushed scarlet. "That will be quite enough! Outside with you this instant!"

Fargo felt a familiar tightness in his throat as he watched Virginia sashay from the premises, her supple bottom swaying in a frank invitation.

"I apologize for her behavior," Ragsdale was saying. "She's always been too headstrong for her own good." He cleared his throat in embarrassment. "Now how about my offer? Are you willing to ride out to the Bar R sometime soon and hear me out?"

Before Skye Fargo quite knew what he was doing, his mouth moved of its own accord. "Why not? I planned on staying here a few days anyway, so I guess it can't hurt." He raised the bottle and noticed his reflection in the mirror, but in his mind's eye all he saw were Virginia Ragsdale's delicious curves. The scent of her perfume hung in the air, promising treasure beyond compare.

"Excellent! You won't regret your decision."

"I hope not," Fargo said, and he had never meant anything more.

WAR EAGLES
BY FRANK BURLESON

In the North, a lanky lawyer named Abraham Lincoln was recovering from a brutal political setback. In the South, eloquent U.S. Senator Jefferson Davis was risking all in a race for governor of his native Mississippi. And far to the Southwest, the future of the frontier was being decided as the U.S. Army, under Colonel Bull Moose Sumner, faced the growing alliance of Native Americans led by the great Mangus Colorados and determined to defend their ancestral lands. For First Lieutenant Nathanial Barrington it was his first test as a professional soldier following orders he distrusted in an undeclared war without conscience or quarter— and his test as a man when he met the Apache woman warrior Jocita in a night lit by passion that would yield to a day of dark decision . . .

from **SIGNET**

TRINITY STRIKE
BY SUZANN LEDBETTER

From the heart of Ireland comes the irrepressible Megan O'Malley, whose own spirit mirrors that of the untamed frontier. With nothing to her name but fierce determination, Megan defies convention and sets out to strike it rich, taking any job—from elevator operator to camp cook—to get out west and become a prospector. In a few short months, she has her very own stake in the Trinity mine—and the attention of more than a few gun-slinging bandits. But shrewd, unscrupulous enemies are lurking, waiting to steal her land—and any kind of courtship must wait. . . .

from Signet

THE BORDER CAPTAINS
BY JASON MANNING

The fledgling United States has survived the Revolutionary War. And with the turn of the new century, settlers are poised to continue their westward thrust through the dark and bloody killing grounds of Kentucky. But in their path stands the British military's might, and an even more menacing and worthy foe—the brilliant, brave and legendary Native American chief Tecumseh. The War of 1812 is about to begin. And in the hands of such American heroes as "Mad" Anthony Wayne, William Henry Harrison, Henry Clay, and Daniel Boone ... with the trigger fingers of a buckskin-clad army ... and in the courage, daring and determination of frontiersman Nathaniel "Flintlock" Jones ... history is to be made, a wilderness to be won, and a spellbinding saga of the American past is to be brought to pulse-pounding, unforgettable life ...

The Border Captains is the second epic historical novel of the Flintlock trilogy, written by the acclaimed author of the *High Country* frontier novels.

from SIGNET

COYOTE RUN
BY DON BENDELL

On one side stood the legendary Chief of Scouts, Chris Colt, with his hair-trigger tempered, half brother Joshua, and the proud young Indian brave, Man Killer. On the other side was a mining company that would do anything and kill anyone to take over Coyote Run, the ranch that the Colts had carved out of the Sangre Cristo Mountains, with their sweat and their blood. Their battle would flame amid the thunder of a cattle drive, the tumult of a dramatic courtroom trial, the howling of a lynch mob, and a struggle for an entire town. And as the savagery mounted, the stakes rose higher and higher, and every weapon from gun and knife to a brave lawyer's eloquent tongue and the strength and spirit of two beautiful women came into powerful play.

from SIGNET

THE DAWN OF FURY
BY RALPH COMPTON

Nathan Stone had experienced the horror of Civil War battlefields. But the worst lay ahead. When he returned to Virginia, to the ruins of what had been his home, his father had been butchered and his mother and sister stripped, ravished, and slain. The seven renegades who had done it had ridden away into the West. Half-starved and afoot, Nathan Stone took their trail. Nathan Stone's deadly oath—blood for blood—would cost him seven long years, as he rode the lawless trails of an untamed frontier. His skill with a Colt would match him equally with the likes of the James and Youngers, Wild Bill Hickok, John Wesley Hardin, and Ben Thompson. Nathan Stone became the greatest gunfighter of them all, shooting his way along the most relentless vengeance trail a man ever rode to the savage end ... and this is how it all began.

from **SIGNET**